Merlin: The Book of Magic

THE WIZARD'S OWN JOURNAL OF
SECRET TREASURES, TERRIBLE FOES,
TRUE FRIENDS, AND MAGICAL WORLDS

Other Books by T. A. Barron

Visit T. A. Barron's website: www.tabarron.com

BOOK 12

Merlin
The Book of Magic

THE WIZARD'S OWN JOURNAL OF
SECRET TREASURES, TERRIBLE FOES,
TRUE FRIENDS, AND MAGICAL WORLDS

T. A. BARRON

illustrated by August Hall

PHILOMEL BOOKS
An Imprint of Penguin Group (USA) Inc.

A companion volume to The Merlin Saga—including
The Lost Years of Merlin epic, The Merlin's Dragon trilogy,
and The Great Tree of Avalon trilogy

Patricia Lee Gauch, Editor

PHILOMEL BOOKS
A division of Penguin Young Readers Group.
Published by The Penguin Group. Penguin Group (USA) Inc., 375 Hudson Street, New York, NY 10014, U.S.A. Penguin Group (Canada), 90 Eglinton Avenue East, Suite 700, Toronto, Ontario M4P 2Y3, Canada (a division of Pearson Penguin Canada Inc.). Penguin Books Ltd, 80 Strand, London WC2R 0RL, England. Penguin Ireland, 25 St. Stephen's Green, Dublin 2, Ireland (a division of Penguin Books Ltd). Penguin Group (Australia), 250 Camberwell Road, Camberwell, Victoria 3124, Australia (a division of Pearson Australia Group Pty Ltd). Penguin Books India Pvt Ltd, 11 Community Centre, Panchsheel Park, New Delhi—110 017, India. Penguin Group (NZ), 67 Apollo Drive, Rosedale, North Shore 0632, New Zealand (a division of Pearson New Zealand Ltd). Penguin Books (South Africa) (Pty) Ltd, 24 Sturdee Avenue, Rosebank, Johannesburg 2196, South Africa. Penguin Books Ltd, Registered Offices: 80 Strand, London WC2R 0RL, England.

Published simultaneously in Canada.
Printed in the United States of America.
Text set in ITC Galliard.

Library of Congress Cataloging-in-Publication Data
Barron, T. A. Merlin : the book of magic / T. A. Barron ; illustrated by August Hall. p. cm. "The wizard's owl journal of secret treasures, terrible foes, true friends, and magical worlds." "A companion volume to The Lost Years of Merlin epic, Merlin's Dragon trilogy, and The Great Tree of Avalon trilogy." Summary: A compendium of maps, character descriptions, magical terms, timelines, and other tidbits from the author's Merlin saga. 1. Merlin (Legendary character)—Juvenile fiction. [1. Merlin (Legendary character)— Fiction. 2. Magic—Fiction. 3. Wizards—Fiction. 4. Fantasy.] I. Hall, August, ill. II. Title. PZ7.B27567Men 2011 [Fic]—dc22 2011013552ISBN 978-0-399-24741-5
3 5 7 9 10 8 6 4

To Merlin, who first introduced himself to me under
an ancient oak tree near Oxford 35 years ago,
and who continues to inspire me
and so many others with his magic.—TAB

To Tom Barron, Patricia Gauch, Semadar Megged,
and Allen Spiegel for giving me the opportunity
to work on a wonderful project.—AH

 Shim the giant tries to hold up the crumbling
Shrouded Castle—certainly, definitely, absolutely.

CONTENTS

 Water dragons! Their enormous bodies
suddenly burst out of the depths.

WARNING
TO THE
READER

Pray, take care with this book! You see, it contains the secret journal of the great wizard Merlin. Over the centuries, others contributed their share—while still others sought to capture Merlin's magic for themselves. Recently, these papers have come to me . . . by strange, magical, and (I must confess) nefarious means.

And now, the secret journal of Merlin has come to *you*. But I must warn you: These pages hold more than knowledge. They hold danger. Sometimes subtle, often surprising, the secrets they contain have taken many centuries, and more than a few lives, to assemble. If these secrets fell into the wrong hands . . . the enemies of magic could use them to destroy, not create. So guard this book with the valor of a wizard!

Just how did these papers come to me, and now to you? I shall reveal that only in summary form—to protect the valiant souls who helped me along the way . . . and to torment the ones who did not. (Yes, I know who you are.)

From the hand of Merlin . . .

Merlin himself gave birth to this book by crafting a simple, leather-bound journal that he closed with a magical clasp. All through the Lost Years of his youth, he wrote in the journal, hiding it deep in the folds of his tunic.

Beginning soon after he had washed ashore from the raging sea, Merlin's earliest entries speak with the voice of a young man who is very far from a great wizard. He is nameless, homeless, and powerless—rife with pain that makes those original entries difficult to read. (And it doesn't help that his handwriting is truly terrible.)

In time, he discovered the magic within him—and added new pages as that magic grew to astonishing levels. The journal expanded as young Merlin learned the secrets of the mist-shrouded isle of Fincayra, as well as the dark truths of his childhood. And it thickened more as he healed a wounded dragon, fell in love, battled creatures who could devour magic, ran with the deer, witnessed the Dance of the Giants, traveled through time to meet his elder self, mastered the Seven Songs, took his sister's spirit into himself, and—at last—learned to see in an entirely new way, a way befitting a wizard.

To Rhia . . .

When Merlin finally left for Earth, hoping to inspire a new realm called Camelot, he tucked the journal into the innermost pocket of his blue cloak. But when he returned to Avalon to marry Hallia, he entrusted the journal to his sister, Rhiannon, soon to become High Priestess. Rhia added several fascinating entries of her own, which range from the first detailed description of light flyers to her horrible premonition that led to the Dark Prophecy. Ultimately, before she vanished mysteriously in the Year of Avalon 413, Rhia hid the journal in a knothole of the ancient oak tree Arbassa in Lost Fincayra.

To Krystallus . . .

Eventually, Merlin and Hallia's only child, Krystallus Eopia, overcame his lack of magic to become Avalon's most famous explorer. On one harrowing journey to Lost Fincayra, he found the journal—now so old that wrinkles creased its leather cover like the face of an old friend. He slipped the journal into his tunic pocket and carried it everywhere. As the first person after Serella, the elf queen, to master the dangerous art of portal-seeking, he discovered many wondrous places. Throughout his adventures, Krystallus noted unusual facts—whether bizarre, beautiful, mysterious, or terrifying.

Whenever he visited the Eopia College of Mapmakers, Krystallus added more notes (as well as maps and drawings) to the journal, increasing its size dramatically. He also tried his best to decipher the chicken scratches of his father's writing. (I have often imagined him in the college library, seated beneath the great stained-glass window that had been melted by fire dragons into the shape of a star within a circle, cursing at Merlin's impossible scrawl.) As a result, Krystallus completed the most extensive portrait ever made of Merlin's magical realms.

For many years, Krystallus guarded the journal with the ferocity of a warrior. Not even Babd Catha, the Ogres' Bane, could have pried it away. Finally, he decided to take it with him as he embarked on his most ambitious journey of all—to find the secret pathway to the stars. Suspecting that he might never return, he hid the journal in a remote place: the Hall of the Heartwood, deep within the trunk of the Great Tree.

To Tamwyn . . .

It was there that Tamwyn, the son Krystallus never knew, discovered the secret journal. Buried in a box, along with a handwritten scroll, these writings seemed to speak right into Tamwyn's mind. His father's entries rang with the man's rumbling voice and thoughtful cadence. As much as Krystallus had prized these papers, this young lad—Merlin's true heir—treasured them even more.

In the tumultuous days that followed, Tamwyn added many notes of his own to the journal. Unfortunately, his hastily scrawled entries are almost as difficult to read as Merlin's. Worse yet, the pages were badly battered, sometimes beyond recognition, during the lad's far-flung travels. Like the pack that carried it, the journal was gnawed by sharp teeth, drenched by Tamwyn's ride on an upward-flowing waterfall, crushed by the claws of the mighty dragon Basilgarrad, and singed by the flames of fire angels during the final battle for Avalon in the stars.

To me . . .

All these factors made reviving this journal a daunting task. When I found it—hidden inside a crystal cave whose location came to me in a dream—it was a tattered pile of shredded leather and crumpled pages. The entries were a complete mess and spanned four separate worlds. But as much as that task challenged me, it also thrilled me. For I knew how far these pages had traveled—from the ancient shores of Fincayra, through the seven root-realms of Avalon, up the uncharted paths of the Great Tree, across the River of Time, and ultimately . . . to the stars.

And now to you.

Along the way, these pages have gained many stains, marks, and tatters, along with a mysterious magic of their own. And so they now come—from the hands of Merlin, Rhia, Krystallus, Tamwyn, and others—to you.

T.A. Barron

P.S. If you would like to learn more about these matters, information is scarce. But you could, I suppose, check The Merlin Saga, which includes these highly unreliable sources: The Lost Years of Merlin, a five-book epic; Merlin's Dragon, a trilogy; and The Great Tree of Avalon, a trilogy.

FINCAYRA
MERLIN'S ENCHANTED ISLE

Strange Characters and Magical Terms

Arbassa

Deep in **Druma Wood** grew a great oak tree whose branches reached so high they brushed the clouds. This was Arbassa—a tree so magical that it became the home as well as the guardian of a very special child: young **Rhia**. Many years later, in memory of this tree and its marvelous forest, Rhia's mother, **Elen**, chose the name Drumadians for the members of the **Society of the Whole**. And for similar reasons, the mysterious **Lady of the Lake** dubbed her home New Arbassa.

When young Rhia first showed Arbassa to the boy who would become **Merlin**, at the start of his **Lost Years**, he described it this way:

From the center of the clearing rose a great oak, mightier than any tree I had ever seen. Its burly branches reached upward from the trunk, so thick that it seemed to be made of several trunks fused together. Set in the midst of those branches, glowing like a giant torch, was an aerial cottage whose beams and walls and windows curled with the twisting limbs. Layers of leaves overlaid the tree house, so that the light radiating from its windows shone through multiple curtains of green. Here, at last, was Arbassa.

Rhia lifted her arms in greeting. In response, the branches of the tree shimmered just enough to drop a light rain of dew on her upturned face.

Aylah, the Wind Sister ᗒ

There was a sudden rush of air and the sweet scent of cinnamon when **Merlin** uncorked an ancient flask. For he'd just rescued one of **Fincayra**'s most remarkable creatures: Aylah, a wishla-haylagon—also known as a wind sister. Trapped inside the flask by the hag **Domnu**, Aylah would surely have died if the young wizard hadn't saved her. As she told him, "I must move as freely as the air itself, Emrys Merlin. For I am made to travel fast and far, never sleeping, never stopping." Whenever she spoke, a warm breeze swept slowly around Merlin, fluttering his tunic, embracing him with wind that carried the scent of cinnamon. Many times during his quest of the **Seven Songs** and his search for the **lost wings**, Aylah appeared and lightly caressed his cheek. Once she even carried him, along with **Rhia** and the jester **Bumbelwy**, all the way across Fincayra to find the spirit of a star, **Gwri of the Golden Hair**. Years later, she reappeared, at the request of **Dagda**, to take an eventful journey with the tiny creature who would become the great dragon **Basilgarrad**. Yet Aylah never stayed long. For she was always as restless as the wind.

Ballymag

"The oddest-looking creature I ever saw" was how **Merlin** described the clawed seal called the Ballymag. Somehow able to survive in **Fincayra**'s deadly **Haunted Marsh**, he always enjoyed a mud bath (a "scrubamuck"), especially when the mud was thick and dark ("so very mooshlovely"). The pinnacle sprite **Nuic** recalls seeing him at Merlin's wedding to **Hallia** atop the highest peak in the Seven Realms in the Year of Avalon 27. But few people know that when the Ballymag first met Merlin, he feared that the young wizard would try to have him "cookpotted and swalloweaten."

Bumbelwy

A jester who can't make anyone laugh? Meet Bumbelwy. When **Merlin** first saw him at **Fincayra**'s Town of Bards, the jester was earnestly trying to be funny. But his hands drooped, his shoulders sagged, and his back stooped. Meanwhile, his entire face down to his chin seemed to frown. Even the bells on his droopy, wide-brimmed hat sounded like a funeral dirge. Yet he called himself Bumbelwy the Mirthful—perhaps because, as the bard **Cairpré** put it, "bread yearns to rise beyond its size."

To Merlin's great annoyance, Bumbelwy joined him on the quest of the **Seven Songs**. The young wizard did everything he could to lose him, but without success. At last, when Merlin was about to be devoured by the dragon **Valdearg**, Bumbelwy sang what he thought was a sorrowful lament, expressing his deep sadness. But unexpectedly, his song made the dragon laugh—allowing Merlin to escape. Ever after, when Merlin himself wanted to laugh, he only needed to recall Bumbelwy's song:

A dragon savors all he eats
But values best the living treats
Who squirm and squeal before they die,
The filling of a dragon's pie.
O dragon, 'tis my friend you eat!
Alas, how sweet the dragon's meat.

The dragon loves the crunch of bones
And all the dying cries and groans
Of people gone without a trace,
Into deep digestive space.
O dragon, 'tis my friend you eat!
Alas, how sweet the dragon's meat.

My friend, in dragon's mouth interred,
Was even robbed his final word.
For down he went into that hole,

His parting sentence swallowed whole.
O dragon, 'tis my friend you eat!
Alas, how sweet the dragon's meat.

Cairpré

"The people's bard" he was called—a poet who understood both the light and dark sides of mortal creatures. As **Elen**'s tutor, he introduced her to the Greek myths; as her lover, he brought her the deepest happiness of her life. Later, as **Merlin**'s mentor, he taught magic and lore—and also helped the young man build his first musical instrument, the time-honored tradition of someone who hoped to become a wizard. Cairpré died too soon, in **Fincayra**'s final battle, his person just as beloved as his poetry. Like his most famous lines, he is remembered wholeheartedly, with both sweetness and sorrow.

Cwen

Part human and part tree, Cwen's gnarled skin looked very much like bark, while her tangled brown hair resembled a mass of vines. Her rootlike feet remained unshod, and she wore no adornment but the silver rings on the smallest of her twelve knobby fingers. Beneath her white robe, she moved like a tree bending with the wind, wafting a scent of spring blossoms. Yet no one could mistake her age: Her back bent like a trunk weighed down by a long winter's snow. For she was, indeed, very old—the last survivor of her people, the treelings.

Cwen was, for many years, **Rhia**'s loyal companion. They lived together in the boughs of the great oak tree **Arbassa** in the heart of **Druma Wood**. Then Cwen succumbed to the temptation of regaining her youth—and betrayed Rhia to a band of **gobsken**. Although Rhia escaped, the two former friends would not meet again until after the **Dance of the Giants**, during **Merlin**'s quest of the **Seven Songs**. By then, Cwen had changed into a butterfly, which helped Merlin to discover his own power of transformation . . . and helped Rhia to forgive her at last. And so it was that, in the early days of **Avalon**, Cwen became one of the first people to join Rhia and **Elen** in the **Society of the Whole**.

Dinatius

Tall and strong, Dinatius lived in the squalid village of Caer Vedwyd, not far from the rock-bound coast of Gwynedd, the ancient name for Wales on **Earth**. He could carry heavy loads— and also survive regular beatings from the village smith who housed him. When he was not stoking the smith's fires, Dinatius cut and carried wood, worked the bellows, and hauled iron ore. Yet he still found time to lead a gang of young ruffians who tormented young **Merlin** and the mysterious woman who sheltered him.

As much as Merlin hated this bully, he dashed into a raging fire to save Dinatius's life. But Merlin didn't learn, until much later, whether he had succeeded. For those very flames destroyed his eyes, forcing him to find a new way to see—a way befitting a wizard. And when Merlin did, at last, discover the truth about Dinatius, it was a wrenching surprise.

Domnu

Beautiful is not the word to describe the ancient hag of **Fincayra**'s dreaded **Haunted Marsh**. She has no hair on her head; her scalp is so wrinkled that it looks like the folds of an exposed brain. One large wart sprouts like a horn from the middle of her forehead. Her mouth is filled with angular, crooked teeth. And her eyes, utterly black, never blink.

Domnu, whose name means *dark fate,* wears a simple robe that resembles a cloth sack with many pockets and always goes barefoot. Yet despite her simple garb, she carries an aura of great power and deep mystery. She is, after all, older than time—and oblivious to the fickle demands of morality. As the bard **Cairpré** described her to young **Merlin** and

> *She is older than time.*

Shim, "Domnu is neither good nor evil, friend nor foe, mortal nor immortal. She simply is." But she does have a merciful side: When she sees how frightened Shim is, she consoles him, "Be not scared. Dying isn't so bad after the first time."

An avid gambler, she loves to place wagers on things she deems worthless, such as dice, chess pieces, or human lives. Piles of objects she uses for games of chance—bones, jewels, spools of yarn, cards, pebbles, shells, and eyeballs—are every-where in her lair; the walls are covered with jumbled calculations, symbols, and runes. When Merlin asks for her help, she grins, showing her misshapen teeth, and replies, "What would you like to wager, my pet?"

Elen of the Sapphire Eyes

No wonder she helped **Merlin** become a man of many worlds and many times: Elen's life bridged **Earth**, **Fincayra**, and **Avalon**. On Earth, she was called Branwen; in Fincayra, she was known as Elen of the Sapphire Eyes; and in Avalon, she became Elen the Founder. Her breadth as a person enabled her to love two very different men—the gentle poet **Cairpré** and the ruthless king **Stangmar**.

Similarly, Elen's spiritual breadth enabled her to draw from several different faiths. Combining the wisdom of Druids, Christians, and Jews, she became a skilled healer as well as a bard, and she had a special fondness for Greek myths. As likely to tell a tale about the healer from Galilee as she was to speak of Moses or Athena, she was respected by the most learned people in her midst—and reviled by the most intolerant. In fact, her son, the young **Merlin**, first called upon his magical powers to save her from being burned at the stake by some of her enemies, a gang of young ruffians led by **Dinatius**. While Merlin did manage to save Elen's life, he started a terrible fire that caused him to lose forever the use of his eyes. In time, with Elen's help, he learned to see in an entirely different, more powerful way—not with his eyes, but with his heart.

Later, when Merlin's magical seed gave birth to the world of Avalon, Elen and her daughter, **Rhia**, founded a new spiritual order: the **Society of the Whole**, dedicated to promoting harmony among all living creatures and to protecting the Great Tree that sustains all life. This new faith, which began as just a gleam in its founder's sapphire eyes, spread rapidly across Avalon. It paid close attention to the seven sacred **Elements**— Earth, Air, Fire, Water, Life, LightDark, and Mystery—which together constitute the Whole. Elen and her followers (including Rhia, **Lleu of the One Ear**, and **Babd Catha**) built their sacred compound in **Stoneroot**. And in the compound's very center stood a Great Temple that was, in fact, the circle of stones from Lost Fincayra known as the **Dance of the Giants**.

When Elen died, in the Year of Avalon 37, creatures everywhere grieved. People of all kinds wore sapphires in her honor. And the great spirit **Dagda** personally guided her spirit all the way to the **Otherworld**. There she could, at last, rejoin her life's greatest love, the bard Cairpré.

Eremon

When young **Merlin** saved a pair of deer—a doe and a stag— from huntsmen's arrows, he met two great friends. For they turned out to be deer people of **Fincayra**'s Mellwyn-bri-Meath clan: **Hallia**, who would become Merlin's lover and lifelong companion, and Eremon, her true hearted brother. Eremon was the first to trust the young man—and the first to call him

Young Hawk. When in human form, Eremon walked with long, loping strides. His feet were bare. Like his sister, he possessed rich brown eyes and the strong chin of the deer people. And like his sister, he knew that the best way to come to know each other was "to circle a story," one of the deer people's oldest traditions.

In time, Eremon saw much of himself in Merlin. That commonality deepened when he asked, "How do you know so much about your faults?"—to which Merlin replied, "That's easy. I have a sister." Finally, Eremon vowed to help Merlin on his quest to save the island from the dragon **Valdearg**—even if Eremon himself did not survive. As the deer man declared, "It is right to help another creature, no matter the shape of his track."

Galator

When young **Merlin** first saw the Galator one night early in his **Lost Years**, the pendant seemed to shine with its own light, not just the moon's. Right away, he noticed that the crystal was deep green, with rivers of violet and blue flowing beneath its surface and glints of red that pulsed with life. Truly, it looked almost like a living eye.

This pendant, once believed to be the last of the fabled **Treasures of Fincayra**, had a long history linking Fincayra with **Avalon**. Its journey connected many key people of both worlds. Worn by **Elen of the Sapphire Eyes**, given to Merlin, prized by **Cairpré**, stolen by **Domnu**, buried in lava during a battle with **kreelixes**, rescued by the great spirit **Dagda**, and carried to Avalon by **Rhia**, this deep green pendant ultimately belonged to the **Lady of the Lake**, her friend **Nuic**, and the young priestess **Elli**. Yet despite its many bearers, only Elli managed to tap its greatest power: to speak with the person she loved, across distances as vast as the sky itself. For the Galator's deepest magic enabled loved ones to see and hear each other beyond any limits of space and time.

Gobsken

Looking for exceptionally good warriors who are also exceptionally bad company? Gobsken are your answer—unless you don't enjoy smelling breath so terrible it could fell an ogre. Gobsken have broad chests, burly limbs, greenish gray skin, and eyes as thin as slits. Their three-fingered hands curl naturally into fists. And they are swift to anger.

> *Vicious fighters who respond to fear, lust, and greed.*

Like their ancient king **Harshna**, gobsken are vicious fighters who respond to fear, lust, and greed. While they are invariably rude, they are often quite clever, as well as persistent. As **Fincayra**'s king **Stangmar** and **Avalon**'s sorcerer **Kulwych** both proved, these qualities make gobsken ideal allies for those who serve the spirit warlord **Rhita Gawr**.

Grand Elusa

This enormous white spider, larger than a horse, lived in the Misted Hills of **Lost Fincayra**. Although her appetite was great—she ate so much that even **living stones** trembled at her approach—her wisdom was also great. That is why she sided with young **Merlin** and **Rhia**, and against the hag **Domnu**, at the Great Council that began the quest of the **Seven Songs**. And that is also why the peoples of that world ultimately chose the Grand Elusa to guard the precious **Treasures of Fincayra**, which included the Flowering Harp, the sword Deepercut, the Caller of Dreams, the Orb of Fire, and six of the Seven Wise Tools. (The seventh Tool, most people believed, had been lost in the **Dance of the Giants** that destroyed **Stangmar**'s **Shrouded Castle**. But Merlin later discovered it.)

Over his long life, Merlin never forgot the great white spider. But he had a different reason: It was in her lair in the Misted Hills that he first encountered the beauty of a **crystal cave**. Quietly, he vowed that one day he, too, would live in a cave of such natural magnificence.

As a gift to the peoples of **Avalon**, the Grand Elusa wove a glistening gown of spider's silk for **Elen of the Sapphire Eyes**. This became the traditional gown of the High Priestess of the **Society of the Whole**. In time, that gown was worn by Elen's daughter, Rhiannon, as well as by **Coerria**. Yet no one loved its graceful design more than a young apprentice third class named **Elliryanna**.

Gwri of the Golden Hair

On the day young **Merlin** met **Rhia** in the **Druma Wood** of **Fincayra**, she led him to the rarest tree in the forest. It was a shomorra tree, whose branches grew every kind of fruit (including purple larkon fruit, which tasted like liquid sunshine). "This is my garden," she explained. Then she showed Merlin a different kind of garden, high above their heads: the garden of the **stars**. Rhia spoke of the wonders of the Fincayran sky—the constellations formed by the dark spaces between the stars, rather than the stars themselves; the **River of Time** that divided past from future; and the star known as Gwri of the Golden Hair.

Later, in the quest of the **Seven Songs**, Rhia and Merlin met the bright-eyed woman who was, to their astonishment, the spirit of that very star. Gwri told them about the power of Leaping across space and time—and gave the young wizard the knowledge he needed to fulfill his dream of living backward in time. Most important, she helped Merlin understand that everything is connected to everything else—because, as she put it, "all voices join in the great and glorious song of the stars." When Gwri vanished at last, she left on **Merlin's staff** the symbol of a star within a circle. Thus was born the symbol for magical travel through space and time—the very symbol that Merlin's son, **Krystallus**, would one day choose for **Avalon**'s famous college of mapmakers.

Gwynnia

When a boulder on the bank of **Fincayra**'s River Unceasing began to quiver, then crack, Gwynnia began her life as a baby dragon. Out from the boulderlike egg she crawled, blinking her triangular, orange eyes that glowed as bright as molten lava. Raising one of her claws, the dragon tried to scratch the yellow bump on her forehead. But she missed and poked the soft, crinkled skin of her nose. She whimpered and shook her head, flapping her blue, bannerlike ears. But when she stopped, her right ear refused to lie flat again. Instead, it stretched out to the side like a misplaced horn. Only the gentle droop at the tip hinted that it was, in fact, an ear.

So began the journey of Gwynnia, daughter of the ferocious dragon **Valdearg**. That journey almost ended moments later, with the terrible murder of her siblings, an attack that left behind only broken shells and hacked bits of dragon flesh. She might well have perished herself—but a young wizard named **Merlin** rescued her, calling on powers he didn't even know he possessed. Then her journey continued, taking her to Valdearg's lair in the Lost Lands, to an enduring friendship with the deer woman **Hallia**, and to a crucial role in the final battle to save Fincayra—a battle that combined **lost wings** and dragon wings.

Hallia (Eo-Lahallia) 🦌

"More lovely than the starry sky, more graceful than the dancing stream." That is how **Merlin** described the deer woman Hallia. Named Eo-Lahallia by her parents, she belonged to the Mellwyn-bri-Meath clan of **Lost Fincayra**. In one tumultuous season, she lost her beloved brother, **Eremon**, and also met Merlin, who would become her closest companion for life. It took some time for Hallia, whose parents had been killed by men who hungered for venison, to trust him. But, in time, this man she called Young Hawk won her confidence, as well as her heart.

Through Hallia, Merlin learned how to run like a deer. She also taught him the deer people's tradition of circling a story, and the truth about the tapestry

> *She taught him about love.*

of tales called the Carpet Caerlochlann. Most important, she taught him about love. When Merlin left Fincayra, his first true home, to travel to the place called **Camelot** on mortal **Earth**, the most painful part of that decision was leaving Hallia. He vowed to come back to her; she promised to listen to the wind every day to hear his footsteps.

And so he returned to **Avalon** in the Year 27 to marry her. They were wed atop the highest peak in the Seven Realms, which the young wizard named Hallia's Peak. Later that year, their son, **Krystallus Eopia**, was born. Many years later, Krystallus would marry **Halona**, and they would have a son of their own: **Tamwyn**. Along with other surprising gifts, this young lad could—thanks to Hallia—run with the speed and grace of a deer.

How did it feel to run that way? Here is how Merlin described it in *The Fires of Merlin*:

> *I heard more sounds than I'd ever known existed. They washed over me in a constant stream—the continual pounding of my own hooves, the echoing reverberations through the soil, and the whispers of a dragonfly's wings. Then I realized that somehow, in a mysterious way, I was listening not just to sounds, but to the land itself. I could hear, not with my ears but with my very bones—the tensing and flexing of the earth under my hooves, the changing flow of the wind, the secret connections among all the creatures who shared these meadows, whether they crawled, slithered, flew, or ran. Not only did I hear them; I celebrated them. For we were bound together as securely as a blade of grass is bound to the soil.*

Kreelixes

Seated under the fabled tree called the Cobbler's Rowan, young **Merlin** finally finished making his first instrument of musical magic: an eight-stringed psaltery. The bard **Cairpré**, along with **Elen** and **Rhia**, watched anxiously as Merlin started to pluck the strings for the first time. Suddenly, a high, piercing shriek sliced through the air like a sword of sound. A dark, winged beast that resembled a giant bat plunged out of the sky—straight at Merlin. A kreelix!

Merlin survived that first attack. But he could never rid himself of the horrid memory of those hooked wings, bloodred mouth, veined ears, and gleaming fangs. He learned that day that even the slightest contact with one of those fangs would destroy the power, as well as the life, of any magical creature. For kreelixes exist for only one purpose: to devour magic in all its forms.

Since ancient times, wizards had avoided battling these magic-eating beasts directly, since they could easily lose their wizard magic. And their lives. Only someone as brave as **Basilgarrad** would ever knowingly confront a kreelix. And weapons such as the magical sword Deepercut couldn't be used. (That sword, in fact, was hidden away for over a hundred years, just so no kreelix could destroy it.) How then could Merlin fight such beasts? That secret, alas, had been lost long before his time. He desperately needed to find it—before the next attack.

Light Flyers

These tiny, luminous creatures are among the rarest in **Fincayra** and **Avalon**. They possess frilled wings that pulse with golden light, enough to illuminate a room. They were made by the mudmakers—people who, in the words of **Aelonnia of Isenwy**, wield "the magic of **Merlin**." It is rumored that dozens of glowing light flyers accompany the **Lady of the Lake** wherever she goes, often perching on her hair.

Living Stones

These flesh-eating boulders are among the most strange—and most dangerous—creatures ever to live in **Fincayra** or **Avalon**. As the young wizard **Merlin** (and many years later, the reckless hoolah **Henni**) discovered, living stones can quickly swallow their prey. They fear no other creature—except the great white spider known as the **Grand Elusa,** who cracks open the stones with the ease of a fox cracking open an egg, and eats up to three at a time when she feels hungry.

No living stone ever had trouble digesting its prey until Merlin came along. When the young wizard fell asleep against a stone, he awoke to find himself entirely consumed. But not digested, for his powerful inner magic prevented that from happening. The living stone coaxed him, "Be stone, young man. Be stone and one with the world." But Merlin refused, insisting, "I am too much alive to become stone! There is so much I want to do—to change, to move, all the things that stones cannot." The creature eventually set Merlin free, but not before it gave him a whole new perspective:

You know so little, young man! A stone comprehends the true meaning of change. I have dwelled deep within the molten belly of a star, sprung forth aflame, circled the worlds in a comet's tail, cooled and hardened over eons of time. I have been smashed by glaciers, seized by lava, swept across undersea plains—only to rise again to the surface upon a flowing river of land. I have been torn apart, cast aside, uplifted and combined with stones of utterly different origins. Lightning has struck my face, quakes have ripped my feet. Yet still I survive, for I am stone.

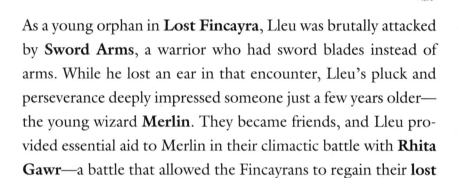

Lleu of the One Ear

As a young orphan in **Lost Fincayra**, Lleu was brutally attacked by **Sword Arms**, a warrior who had sword blades instead of arms. While he lost an ear in that encounter, Lleu's pluck and perseverance deeply impressed someone just a few years older— the young wizard **Merlin**. They became friends, and Lleu provided essential aid to Merlin in their climactic battle with **Rhita Gawr**—a battle that allowed the Fincayrans to regain their **lost wings**.

After the world of **Avalon** sprouted from Merlin's magical seed, Lleu of the One Ear followed **Elen** and **Rhia** in founding the **Society of the Whole**. He became one of Elen's first disciples, joined by **Cwen**, last of the treelings, and (to the astonishment of many who had seen her fiercely attack enemies) **Babd Catha, the Ogres' Bane**. Lleu joined Rhia and Merlin in an extraordinary journey inside the Great Tree, in the Year of Avalon 131, which led to the Drumadians' discovery of **élano**—the essential life-giving sap of the Tree and a source of unfathomable power. Based on this experience, Lleu of the One Ear wrote his masterwork, *Cyclo Avalon,* which describes the workings of élano as well as the seven sacred **Elements** and the **portals** throughout Avalon. For centuries, this book remained the primary text for all Drumadians.

Lost Wings

Long ago, in the earliest days of **Fincayra**, men and women could fly. Though mortal, they had "the wings of angels," as young **Merlin** learned from the bard **Cairpré**. What happened to those wings? Why were they lost? That mystery stayed with Merlin throughout his **Lost Years**, as tormenting as the perpetual ache between his shoulder blades. To solve the mystery, the young wizard needed to journey to the **Forgotten Island**—and to the source of his own deepest fears. At last he succeeded, in the adventure called *The Wings of Merlin,* and won glorious wings of his own. Then he surprised even **Dagda** by offering to give them to an enemy. For Merlin understood that, by doing so, he would gain more than he would lose.

Lost Years

Merlin's Lost Years were the crucial formative years of his youth, kept secret for centuries. During those years, Merlin grew from age twelve to seventeen—and changed dramatically, from a half-drowned boy who washed ashore on a strange coast to a masterful young wizard. At the beginning of those years, he was a homeless, nameless lad with no clue about his past or future. By the end, he was well on his way to becoming the mage of **Camelot**, the mentor of **King Arthur**, and the greatest wizard of all times.

Although he would ultimately make his home on **Earth**, the world of **Fincayra**—where he spent his Lost Years—claimed most of Merlin's youth. And also, perhaps, his heart. For Fincayra rose out of the ocean mist to welcome him; Fincayra helped him discover his magic as well as his deepest passions; and Fincayra gave birth to another magical realm—**Avalon**, which sprouted from a seed planted by Merlin himself. During his years on Fincayra, Merlin learned his greatest lessons: the wonders of Nature, the **Seven Songs of Wizardry**, the importance of seeing beneath the surface of things, and the remarkable power of love. And during those years, he gained many of his life's dearest friends—including **Rhia**, **Trouble**, **Cairpré**, **Hallia**, **Eremon**, **Elen**, and **Shim**. Small wonder, then, that when Merlin finally saved Fincayra, he shuddered at the thought of ever leaving it. For the world of his Lost Years had become his first true home.

Merlin (Olo Eopia)

Long ago, on a remote and rugged coast, a half-drowned boy washed ashore. The sea had robbed him of everything he'd once known. He had no memory, no idea at all who he was. He didn't even know his own name. When he first opened his eyes to the sight of the sea, the rocky shore, and the screeching gulls overhead, no one could have possibly convinced him that he would survive that day to become a wizard. Yet he would, in fact, become Merlin: the person celebrated in three worlds—**Fincayra**, **Avalon**, and **Earth**—as the greatest wizard of all times.

During the **Lost Years** of his youth, Merlin gained much—and also lost much. Along with his dear friends **Rhia**, the hawk **Trouble**, and the giant **Shim**, he witnessed the **Dance of the Giants**. He solved the mystery of the **Seven Songs**, regained the **lost wings** of Fincayra's people, traveled through a magical Mirror to meet his future self, and (thanks to his beloved **Hallia**) learned to run with the grace and speed of a deer. He encountered the wise and peaceful spirit **Dagda**, and became a lifelong enemy of the warrior spirit **Rhita Gawr**. In time, he found his mother, **Elen**, his father, **Stangmar**, and his mentor, the bard **Cairpré**. And he also learned, through painful struggle, the difference between sight and insight. Along the way, he discovered that he possessed both the dark and the light—just as he held other qualities that might seem opposites: youth and age, male and female, mortal and immortal. At last, Merlin won his true name—Olo Eopia, "great man of many worlds, many times." It is a name, as Dagda told him at the moment of Avalon's birth, for someone who is truly complete, just as the cosmos is complete.

Before departing for Earth—where he would become the famous mage of **Camelot** and the mentor of a young king named **Arthur**—Merlin planted a magical seed. That seed grew into a tree so vast that it became a world of its own: the Great Tree of Avalon, home to people as diverse as **Tamwyn** and **Elli**, **Scree** and **Gwirion**, **Palimyst** and **Basilgarrad**. Merlin often returned to Avalon, sometimes in disguise. Yet even when he left that world for many years, his influence remained. That could be said, as well, for Merlin's other home, the mortal realm of Earth.

Nimue

When **Merlin** battled this sorceress in the **Haunted Marsh** of **Fincayra**, he was trying to save the magical Mirror that had revealed his future. And more: He was fighting to save his own destiny. For he had just met someone from the distant future—someone he had never expected to meet—who had told him how to avoid being trapped forever by Nimue in a **crystal cave** on **Earth**.

As Nimue smirked at him malevolently, Merlin thought how much she had changed from the apple-cheeked girl he had met years before in **Pluton**'s bakery during the quest of the **Seven Songs**. Yet perhaps only her outward appearance had changed. For during Pluton's explanation of the magic of Naming, she had tried to steal **Merlin's staff**. And now, in the Haunted Marsh, she again wanted that staff . . . as well as his life.

It would take more than the young wizard's emerging powers to prevail. It would take the love of the deer woman **Hallia**, the loyalty of the dragon **Gwynnia**, and the surprising gratitude of marsh ghouls—whose arrows could douse the light of day. And it would take one thing more: the help of Merlin's disobedient shadow.

Ohnyalei, the staff of Merlin

When young **Merlin** gained his staff from a magical hemlock tree in the **Druma Wood** of **Lost Fincayra**, he couldn't have guessed what awesome power it would one day possess. Yet even as the staff's magic grew, it never lost its original sweet yet tart fragrance of hemlock. That smell, more than anything else, always reminded Merlin of his first true home.

In the course of its adventures with Merlin, the staff acquired seven runes through the help of **Tuatha**—symbolizing the **Seven Songs of Wizardry**, the greatest ideas the young wizard needed to master. The runes depict a butterfly, for the power of Changing; a pair of soaring hawks, for Binding; a cracked stone, for Protecting; a sword, for Naming; a star within a circle, for Leaping; a dragon's tail, for Eliminating; and an eye, for Seeing. While the staff was in Fincayra, the runes glowed with an eerie blue light; in **Avalon**, that color shifted to green.

Tall and gnarled, with a knotted top, the staff rarely left Merlin's side. In time, it gained surprising power, even wisdom, of its own. Merlin believed that it contained an extraordinary concentration of **élano**, the life-giving sap of the Great Tree. He decided to call it Ohnyalei, which means *spirit of grace* in the Fincayran old tongue. Many years later, he was counting on its wisdom when he entrusted it to a young eagleboy named **Scree**. For there could be no separating the fates of the staff, of Merlin's true heir, and of Avalon itself.

Olwen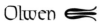

So much did the mer woman Olwen love the wizard **Tuatha**, in the ancient days of **Fincayra**, that she decided to leave her people as well as her ancestral home in order to be with him. This took great courage. It is said that the mer people initially scorned her for this decision, but ultimately came to respect the power of her love. Centuries later, they honored Olwen's memory by creating a miraculous bridge across the sea to help her grandson **Merlin**. This bridge not only saved Merlin's life; it enabled him to solve at last the riddle of his people's **lost wings**.

Because of Olwen's enduring compassion, Tuatha finally agreed to assist Merlin in the quest of the **Seven Songs**. Through that quest, Merlin's staff **Ohnyalei** gained remarkable powers. And Merlin himself gained the wisdom that would allow him, one day in the future, to obtain a magical seed that beat like a heart—a seed that would ultimately grow into the **Great Tree of Avalon**.

Pluton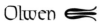

If the stature of bakers is measured in the size of their waistlines, Breadmaster Pluton of **Fincayra** would be enormous on both counts. This plump, ruddy-cheeked fellow was filling his pitcher from the town's unique bread fountain, as he had every day for many years, when he saw young **Merlin** do something nearly impossible: convince two hungry, ill-mannered boys to share a loaf of molasses bread. (Merlin had merely suggested that they each take turns having a bite—or he would eat the loaf himself.) Impressed, Pluton invited Merlin to learn about bread baking—which, the young man soon discovered, was a useful way to learn about life.

"Know your ingredients." That was Pluton's first rule. It guided Merlin in preparing his first heart bread—and in stopping the thievery of a girl named **Nimue**. And it led the young wizard to comprehend the power of Naming, one of the **Seven Songs of Wizardry**. In doing so, Merlin found the sword that he would carry throughout his **Lost Years**, a sword that he would not part with until much later—when he would place it in a stone for young **King Arthur** of **Camelot**.

Rhiannon (Rhia)

Rhia's childhood changed abruptly when, as an infant, she was lost in the **Druma Wood** of **Lost Fincayra**. Adopted by a great oak tree named **Arbassa**, Rhia learned to speak the languages of trees, rivers, and stones. And she learned, as well, the importance of simply listening. When, at the age of twelve, she met her lost brother, she joined him at the **Dance of the Giants** and ultimately helped him to banish **Rhita Gawr** from their world. She also gave her brother his new name: **Merlin**. In their adventures to come, she would give him something even more important—a kind of feminine wisdom that would enable him to inspire many worlds.

Together with her mother, **Elen**, Rhia created the **Society of the Whole** to guide the peoples of **Avalon**. The Society (whose priestesses and priests were called Drumadians, in honor of Druma Wood) was founded on two fundamental principles. The first principle was that all creatures should live together in harmony and mutual respect; the second,

> *She gave her brother his name: Merlin.*

that people should work to protect the Great Tree, which sustains all forms of life. After Elen's death, Rhia became High Priestess of the Society. After a remarkable voyage with Merlin and **Lleu of the One Ear** into the inner depths of the Great Tree (in the Year of Avalon 131), Rhia introduced her followers to **élano**, a source of unfathomable power.

During the struggles of the War of Storms, Rhia grew disillusioned by the increasing arrogance and rigidity of the Drumadians. Finally, after trying unsuccessfully to return the Society to its spiritual roots, she resigned as High Priestess. She departed abruptly, to the grief of her closest friends. What ultimately became of her remains a mystery. It is said that not even Rhia's loyal **maryth**, the pinnacle sprite **Nuic**, or the wise **Lady of the Lake** knew just where she went. She may have traveled to mortal **Earth** to rejoin Merlin. Or perhaps she simply wandered alone through Avalon, unrecognized, and at her death, unmourned.

Seven Songs of Wizardry

Desperately hoping to save the life of his mother, **Elen**, the young wizard **Merlin** traveled from the **Shore of the Speaking Shells** to the great tree **Arbassa** to find these magical runes. As he struggled to decipher them, he heard in his mind the voice of **Tuatha**, who declared:

> *The Seven Songs of Wizardry,*
> *One melody and many,*
> *May guide ye to the Otherworld,*
> *Though hope ye have not any.*

At last, Merlin discovered that these songs revealed the essence of wizardry: The soul of each song held the wisdom he most needed. (The Seven Songs, by virtue of their magic, are different for every person who reads them. They provide the essential truths each person requires to become a wizard.)

Merlin had been warned that he must master all seven before attempting to find the secret pathway to the **Otherworld**—his only hope of saving his mother. Alas, he disregarded that warning. And so, although he learned a little about the powers of Changing, Binding, Protecting, Naming, Leaping, Eliminating, and Seeing—he needed the help of **Rhia** to learn the most important lesson of all.

Shim

Though he stood only as high as a man's knee, smaller than even the smallest dwarf, Shim always insisted that he was really a giant. Of course, no one believed him. Then, at last, he became (in his words) "as tall as the highliest tree"—to which he often added, "Certainly, definitely, absolutely!"

In **Fincayra**'s most tumultuous years, he was a close companion of the young wizard **Merlin**—along with **Rhia** and the brave hawk **Trouble**. In those **Lost Years**, Shim helped them destroy the terrible **Shrouded Castle** and outwit the evil warlord **Rhita Gawr** in the battle known as the **Dance of the Giants**. His adventures with Merlin continued long after the Fincayran people won back their **lost wings** and the world of **Avalon** was born. Shim the giant became famous in story and song.

Then everything changed. During the Battle of the Withered Spring, in the Year of Avalon 498, Shim accidentally saved the life of another giant, **Bonlog Mountain-Mouth**, when he tripped and fell on top of the warriors attacking her. Deeply grateful, Bonlog (the eldest daughter of the giant sorceress Jubolda) tried to thank him with a kiss. But at the sight of her enormous, slobbery mouth, Shim shrieked in terror and fled into the highlands. The humiliated Bonlog angrily pursued him, searching for Shim over many years without success.

Although he escaped Bonlog Mountain-Mouth, Shim met a new misfortune: For reasons he couldn't explain, he began to shrink. When he finally emerged from hiding, he'd returned to his original tiny size—"utterly shrunkelled," as he wailed miserably. Although his bulbous nose still made him recognizably Shim, few people even noticed him. When he finally encountered the elf **Brionna**, he seemed to be nothing more than a small, white-haired dwarf who was very hard of hearing. Yet she managed to recognize him—certainly, definitely, absolutely.

Stangmar

A strong, proud young man who enjoyed riding horseback and climbing trees, Stangmar fell in love with **Elen of the Sapphire Eyes**, a woman from **Earth** who had voyaged to his magical realm. In time, he won her heart and convinced her to stay in **Fincayra**, the world in between mortal and immortal. Though he had struggled as the nonmagical son of a powerful wizard named **Tuatha**, Stangmar strove to become a great leader as king of Fincayra.

Life, however, soon changed for the worse. Not long after Elen gave birth to their children, **Merlin** and **Rhia**, Rhia disappeared into **Druma Wood**, and Stangmar was corrupted by the spirit lord **Rhita Gawr**. Soon Stangmar became merely a pawn in Rhita Gawr's plans to conquer Fincayra. When the evil spirit commanded that the king must murder his son, Stangmar reluctantly agreed. But before he could kill young Merlin, the boy escaped with Elen, traveling to the realm of Britannia on Earth. That journey ended with Merlin washing ashore, nameless and homeless—the event that marked the beginning of his **Lost Years**.

In time, Merlin returned to Fincayra, the land of his birth.

Despite his rage at Stangmar, he saved his father at the collapse of the **Shrouded Castle** during the **Dance of the Giants**. Several years later, after Stangmar had escaped from prison, the former tyrant finally redeemed himself: He sacrificed his own life to save Elen's. In doing so, he enabled Merlin to forgive him at last.

Sword Arms

This terrible warrior wore a horned skull as a mask—and bore two deadly swords instead of arms. He appeared at the worst possible time, while young **Merlin** raced to save his beloved **Fincayra** from conquest by **Rhita Gawr** and labored to solve the mystery of the **lost wings**. Worse yet, this warrior began ruthlessly attacking young orphans. Across the island, parentless children were maimed or worse by this powerful foe.

Merlin had no idea who this brutal warrior might be, or why he would seek out children such as the lad who would one day be called **Lleu of the One Ear**. But Merlin vowed to stop the carnage, even if it kept him from his other goals. When, at last, he confronted Sword Arms in battle, he discovered that any weapon he hurled at the warrior came right back with equal force. To save the children, and to find some way to defeat the warrior, Merlin sailed to the **Forgotten Island**—using the giant **Shim**'s hat as a boat. Thanks to the mer people who came to his aid, perhaps in memory of his grandmother **Olwen**, Merlin landed on the forbidden shore. There he won the final battle with Sword Arms—and discovered the warrior's true identity. Some might call that victory a miracle; others might say the same about the Forgotten Island's return to its ancient shore. Yet the greatest miracle of that day was performed not by Merlin, but by the children he had saved.

T'eilean and Garlatha

How could a small green oasis survive in the midst of **Stangmar**'s terrible Blight on the land of **Fincayra**? Young **Merlin** discovered that it was the orchard and garden of an old married couple: T'eilean and Garlatha. As they emerged from their earthen hut that was supported—almost embraced—by the surrounding trees, the elderly couple moved with an odd, disjointed rhythm. One back straightened as the other curved; one head lifted as the other drooped. As different as their motions were, they seemed unalterably connected. So it did not surprise Merlin or his companion **Shim** (who was, at this time, still very small) that the pair had been married for sixty-eight years. It also did not surprise Merlin that, when T'eilean got the number of years wrong, his wife swiftly corrected him—and gave him a kick in the shin, as well.

Given the dangerous times, it took a while before the travelers felt free to trust these people, whose kindly appearance might have been a disguise. (Shim, when asked his name, replied, "My name is a secret. Nobodily knows it. Not even me.") But in time, trust came. Merlin told them that they reminded him of **Elen**'s tale about Baucis and Philemon, an old couple whose sole wish was to die together—a wish the gods granted by turning them into a pair of trees whose leafy branches would wrap around each other for all time.

None of them could have guessed that the two old gardeners would, in fact, end their days in much the same way. Just as they could not have guessed that, before that end came, they would share several adventures—including caring for the Flowering Harp, one of the great **Treasures of Fincayra**. Yet T'eilean did guess that Merlin might be more than he seemed: "I don't know who you are, young man. But I suspect that, like one of our seeds, you hold surprises within you." At that, Garlatha touched Shim's little head and added, "The same could be said for you, little fellow."

Treasures of Fincayra

For centuries, the Treasures belonged to the people of **Fincayra**, a shared heritage that benefited the land and all its creatures. What did these fabled Treasures include? The Flowering Harp, whose music could bring springtime to any meadow or hillside; the sword Deepercut, which had two edges—one that could cut right into the soul, and one that could heal any wound; the Orb of Fire that possessed what the great spirit **Dagda** called "a force of life" strong enough to rekindle hope even in the darkest times; and the Seven Wise Tools, including a plow that could till its own field, a saw that would cut only as much wood as someone needed, and a hoe that knew how to nurture its seeds. (During the tumultuous **Dance of the**

Giants, one of the Seven Wise Tools was lost. But young **Merlin** and the deer woman **Hallia** later found its location—as well as its secret purpose—in the adventure known as *The Mirror of Merlin*.) There were other Treasures, as well: the fearsome Cauldron of Death, the Caller of Dreams that could bring any dream to life, and one more called "the Last Treasure"—whose identity remained a secret.

> *For centuries, the Treasures belonged to the people of Fincayra.*

Stangmar, the wicked king of the **Shrouded Castle** who had sworn allegiance to the warlord **Rhita Gawr**, tried to capture all the Treasures to enhance his own power. Though his favorite was the Cauldron of Death, he also twisted the power of the Caller of Dreams to silence forever the voices of the people from Caer Neithan, the Town of Bards. In time, he found all the Treasures—except for the Last Treasure. Most people believed that it was a mysterious pendant, the **Galator**. But as Merlin, **Rhia**, and **Shim** ultimately discovered, the Last Treasure was really something quite different.

Trouble

This bold hawk with fire-bright eyes and deadly talons made up for his small size with sheer ferocity and feistiness—and proved so loyal to **Merlin** that many people consider him to be the very first **maryth**. The young man had saved his life in the

Druma Wood of **Lost Fincayra**, even though the hawk caused enough problems to earn the name Trouble.

In the ultimate confrontation with the spirit lord **Rhita Gawr** at the **Shrouded Castle**, Trouble played a crucial role. For this small hawk with the great heart gave his own life to save the lives of Merlin, **Rhia**, and **Shim**—which led to the victory of the **Dance of the Giants**. In the years that followed, Merlin saw Trouble in spirit form only three times: during his visit to the **Otherworld** in search of the Elixir of **Dagda**, his final battle to save Fincayra and restore the **lost wings**, and his wedding to **Hallia**. Yet Merlin's affection for the hawk never diminished. Some believe that, in honor of Trouble, he chose to carry a hawk or an owl wherever he went on **Earth**. And no one doubts that his name was inspired by the merlin hawk who was such a true friend.

Tuatha

Long before **Merlin**'s birth, the wizard Tuatha ruled **Fincayra** with wisdom, but also with unbending severity. He was most stern with his only son, **Stangmar**, who had not inherited any of the wizard's magical powers. Only many years later, when his grandson Merlin visited Tuatha's grave in a dark and eerie glade, did the elder wizard's spirit show any compassion. Maybe that was the influence of Tuatha's wife, **Olwen**, a mer woman who loved him so much that she chose to leave her people and her home beneath the sea just to be with him. Or maybe Tuatha finally recognized his own frailties.

Whatever his reasons, Tuatha finally agreed to help young Merlin find the Elixir of **Dagda** in the **Otherworld**, the only hope of saving Merlin's mother, **Elen**. Although he spoke with characteristic gruffness, Tuatha explained the first crucial step in solving the riddle of the **Seven Songs of Wizardry**. And as a parting gift, Tuatha gave some new magic to Merlin's staff, **Ohnyalei**—magic so powerful that it still radiated from the staff a thousand years later in **Avalon**.

Urnalda

All the dwarves of **Fincayra** feared this enchantress with wild red hair, torch-bright eyes, and earrings of dangling shells that clinked whenever she moved. Sometimes, in a fit of temper, she used her magic to shorten the stubby legs of dwarves who questioned her decisions—or, even worse, to make their precious beards disappear. Yet she successfully guided her people through the Blight of **Stangmar**, ensuring their survival in tunnels deep below the surface.

When **Merlin** first met Urnalda, he felt more like her prisoner than her guest. She glared down at him from her throne of carved jade, stole his staff, and insulted him relentlessly. Later, she destroyed his instrument of musical magic and even tried to rob him of his wizard's powers. Yet despite such behavior, Urnalda remained loyal to the great spirit **Dagda**, and above all, to the survival of the dwarves. That is why Merlin decided she could be his ally . . . if she didn't kill him first.

Valdearg, Wings of Fire

The last and most feared of a long line of emperor dragons, Valdearg blackened much of **Fincayra** with his fiery breath. At the height of his power, he incinerated whole forests and swallowed entire villages—and earned the name Wings of Fire.

Finally, the powerful wizard **Tuatha**, grandfather of **Merlin**, drove the dragon back to his lair in Fincayra's Lost Lands. After a prolonged conflict, the Battle of Bright Flames, the wizard prevailed. Valdearg succumbed to an enchantment of sleep. Why didn't Tuatha simply kill the dragon, as many urged? The wizard had his reasons, though subtle, which he set down in a poem called "The Dragon's Eye." But by the time young Merlin first arrived on the isle of Fincayra, the poem had been forgotten; only a few bards, such as **Cairpré**, could remember any of it. Valdearg, meanwhile, remained in his flame-seared hollow, slumbering fitfully.

Until he awoke—more wrathful than ever. No dragon of the past had ever possessed such a deadly combination of power and intelligence. And no dragon of the future would rival him, either—at least not for centuries, until **Avalon**'s two greatest dragons would appear: **Basilgarrad**, mighty lord of the sky; and **Hargol**, emperor of the waters. When Valdearg awoke, only one creature could quell his rage. And that was **Gwynnia**, his lost child.

Wondrous Places

Crystal Cave

Glowing crystals! The walls, ceiling, and floor of this cave radiated and danced with color. Crystals sparkled and flashed all around us, as if the light shining on a rippling river had been poured into the very earth. And I am quite sure that my own face glowed as well, for even in the days when I could see with my own eyes, when colors ran deeper and light shone brighter, I had never seen anything as beautiful as this crystal cave.

So **Merlin** described the crystal cave of the **Grand Elusa**. Of all the wondrous places on the isle of **Fincayra**, none made a deeper impression on the young wizard. No wonder that, many years later in **Earth**'s realm of **Camelot**, he sought to find his own crystal cave.

Dance of the Giants

Signifying both the climactic battle in the Dark Hills of **Lost Fincayra** and the place where that battle occurred, the Dance of the Giants saw the destruction of the **Shrouded Castle** and the end of **Stangmar**'s brutal reign. The battle also ensured Fincayra's well-being, thanks to the bravery of the hawk **Trouble**, by sending the spirit lord **Rhita Gawr** back to the **Otherworld**. Centuries later, bards still sing about the sacrifice of Trouble, the heroism of young **Merlin** and **Rhia**, and the unexpected bravery of a small fellow named **Shim**—who hurled himself into the Cauldron of Death to save the lives of his friends. In doing so, Shim fulfilled Fincayra's most mysterious prophecy and revived the giants, Fincayra's most ancient people. At the same time, his bravery transformed him into a giant—which proved the truth of the **Grand Elusa**'s observation that "bigness means more than the size of your bones."

And so, in this battle, Fincayra was saved, the lost **Treasures** found, and a young wizard's memory restored. That same young wizard gained the name Merlin, inspired by the merlin hawk who had given his all. The crumbled remains of the Shrouded Castle took a new name, as well: Its ring of mammoth stones, standing in a stately circle, became *Estonahenj*, meaning *Dance of the Giants* in the land's most ancient tongue.

Years later, the great spirit **Dagda** helped the followers of **Elen** transport the circle of stones to the new world of **Avalon**. Rebuilt in **Stoneroot**, it became the Great Temple in the center of the compound dedicated to the **Society of the Whole**.

Within that circle, a thousand years later, a young apprentice priestess named **Elli** would often meditate, wondering what marvels those stones had witnessed.

Druma Wood

Home to young **Rhia**, and to the great oak **Arbassa** that sheltered her in its branches, this deep forest held wonder, magic, and an astounding diversity of life. It was here that Rhia taught **Merlin** how to speak the languages of rivers, trees, and stones. And it was here that **Elen**, at the very edge of death, drank the Elixir of **Dagda,** which allowed her to survive. So great was Elen's gratitude to this place—and so great was the power of Nature that it contained—she chose the name Drumadians for members of the **Society of the Whole**, the guiding force in the new world of **Avalon**.

Fincayra (Lost Fincayra)

This mist-shrouded isle teemed with wondrous places. Here one could find the **Druma Wood**, in whose glades lived **Rhia**, the **Grand Elusa**, and the ancient tree **Arbassa**. The legendary Carpet Caerlochlann, made from the misty threads of story, was woven on the island's shores. **Varigal**, the original home of the giants, rose from the highest mountains. The Town of Bards, where the beloved poet **Cairpré** composed, often rang with story and song. Far to the north, the mysterious **Otherworld** Well, pathway to the spirit realm, lay hidden. And the **Haunted Marsh** held treasures as great as a Mirror of destiny—and dangers as great as the hag **Domnu**.

The Isle of Fincayra was, like **Avalon**, a world between worlds. Part mortal, part immortal, Fincayra was the first true home of young **Merlin**—and the place he lived during his **Lost Years**. It was also home to some of the first citizens of Avalon: **Elen of the Sapphire Eyes**, who founded the **Society of the Whole**; the wise young woman Rhiannon, who taught Merlin the languages of trees, rivers, and stones; **Lleu of the One Ear**, who became a scholar of **élano**; and **Shim**, who had the heart of a true giant.

For many years, a terrible Blight spread across the isle. When, at last, Fincayra was saved, it was also lost. For with the defeat of **Rhita Gawr** and the return of the **lost wings** came the island's ultimate merging with the spirit realm. Thick vapors began to flow over Fincayra, bubbling out of its very soil. Slowly the land withdrew into the Otherworld, leaving only the mist behind. But something different happened in the region once called the **Forgotten Island**—the place where Merlin had planted a magical seed that beat like a heart. From that seed, a Great Tree sprouted, ensuring that its roots would be anchored forever in the mists of Lost Fincayra.

W · E
S

LOS

THE

Ruins of Varigal *be there giants?*

Lake of the Face

living stones

Tuatha's Grave

dwarves last seen here

crossing

Crystal Cave of the Grand Elusa

orchards

THE MISTED HILLS

Cobblers' Rowan

Arbassa, Home of Rhia

The River Unceasing

DRUMA WOOD

Treelings once lived here

The Last Shomorra

shore of the speaking shells

Trouble found here

Forgotten Island

dunes

Emrys' Landing

I·SCHOENHERR·MCMXCVI

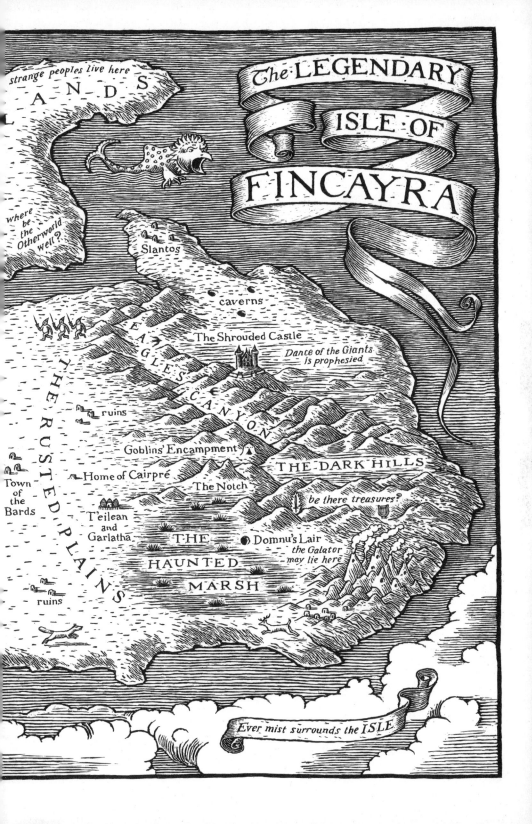

Forgotten Island

Far to the west of **Fincayra**'s rugged Faro Lanna coast, there sat an island, dark and mysterious. During **Merlin**'s quest of the **Seven Songs**, that island both attracted and repulsed him. And for good reason: The Forgotten Island held both the greatest mystery and the gravest danger of his **Lost Years**. Only when, thanks to the miraculous bridge of the mer people, he finally reached the island's shores, would he learn the truth about the **lost wings**, the power of forgiveness, and his own destiny. For in that moment, just as the ancient prophecy had foretold, "the land long forgotten could return to its shore."

Haunted Marsh ⤚

The most terrifying place in all of **Fincayra**, the Haunted Marsh held deadly marsh ghouls, the hag **Domnu**, and many more dangers that only nightmares could describe. Yet the steaming bogs also hid surprises of different kinds, including the "mooshlovely" lair of the **Ballymag**, the secret of the seventh Wise Tool, and the magical Mirror that could show young **Merlin** his future—a future he never expected.

The origins of the Haunted Marsh are as obscure as the vapor-shrouded land itself. Yet many bards, including Merlin's mentor **Cairpré**, believed that, long ago, this area was home to a community of enchantresses known as the Xania-Soe. These women lived secretly but also peacefully, amassing great wealth not in jewels or coins or weapons, but in knowledge. So great was their wisdom that, it was said, the wind itself refused to blow through their region, to avoid spreading dangerous knowledge to other lands. The enchantresses even learned how to bend time in a magical Mirror. Most amazing of all, they discovered how to coax wondrous perfumes from the flowers of their meadows, so that the air of their realm was always fragrant with magic.

When the warlord **Rhita Gawr** learned of their vast power, he tried to conquer them. And he very nearly succeeded. Just when his army was about to invade, the enchantresses realized that all was lost—and chose to make a terrible sacrifice. To repel the attack, they threw a curse upon their beloved homeland—a curse that made their magical flowers spew poisonous vapors into the air. Because no wind ever blew there, the poisons

A Detail of THE HAUNTED MARSH

To EAGLES' CANYON

Beware the Sorceress

To THE DARK HILLS

The Mists of Time lurk within the Mirror

To THE RUSTED PLAINS

The Flaming Tree

The Lair of Domnu

Giants' Pathway

Be there Queljies?

Ector's Hiding

Tunnels of Thorns

Deadly Beetles

village

Marsh Ghouls be here?

Ballymag's Cave

To the Region of

THE SMOKING CLIFFS

IAN SCHOENHERK MCMXCIX

The Troubled Forest

Heed well the warnings of the trees

settled into the land itself, twisting all life into death, all light into shadow. Despite their rage and grief, the enchantresses refused to leave their long-cherished home. Soon they transformed into deadly, ghoulish beings—the marsh ghouls. And so they continued to guard their territory, feeling only sorrow and wrath, bringing revenge to all who came near. Only one person—the young Merlin—ever dared to hope that, somehow, the marsh ghouls might still recall their better selves . . . and rise to help save Fincayra.

Shore of the Speaking Shells

A half-drowned boy washed ashore on this beach—and changed the destiny of **Fincayra**. For that boy was **Merlin**. Amazed by the intensity of this world's colors, so much richer and deeper than those of **Earth**, he began to explore. And he discovered the ominous whispers of an ancient shell, whispers that warned of his doom. Later, he returned to this very beach in the quest of the **Seven Songs**, hoping to find Washamballa, sage among the shells. The shell's watery voice poured over Merlin's mind like an endless wave—and told him what he must do to save the life of his mother, **Elen**.

Shrouded Castle

Rhia and **Merlin** both shuddered when they learned about the Shrouded Castle—the dreaded home of **Fincayra**'s wicked king **Stangmar**, his deathless ghoul-iants, and the spirit warlord **Rhita Gawr**. Yet they needed to go there, if they were to save the island from destruction. That castle held not only their enemies, but the precious **Treasures of Fincayra**. So they began their journey, which—thanks to the bravery of two small warriors, **Trouble** and **Shim**—led to the remarkable **Dance of the Giants**.

> *The dreaded home of Fincayra's wicked king Stangmar.*

How did this castle come to exist? That is a story best told by its stones. For those stones were hewn by teams of giants, and then assembled into a temple to celebrate the great spirits **Dagda** and **Lorilanda**. Infused with magic by the **Grand Elusa**, the vast stone temple turned ceaselessly on its foundation: an unending prayer to the circle of life. The temple continued to turn for centuries, guarded by men and women of deep faith. Then Stangmar, aided by Rhita Gawr, saw its value as a fortress. They stormed the temple and made it their own. They caused fumes to pour from the windows, completely shrouding the edifice. Rather than simply slaying the guards, Rhita Gawr used his twisted magic to change them into ghouliants—warriors whose lives would end only when the castle stopped spinning. And that could only happen if Fincayra's giants returned and danced within the walls that they had built so long ago.

Smoking Cliffs ⤸

In the far southeastern part of **Fincayra** lay the ancient home of the deer people, the Mellwyn-bri-Meath clan. **Hallia** and **Eremon** from the clan taught **Merlin**, whom they called Young Hawk, many secrets of their people—including the legend of the Carpet Caerlochlann, which was woven from the threads from countless stories. Eremon showed Merlin how to become a deer and how to find the legendary Wheel of Wye; Hallia showed him how to circle a story, how to find the seventh Wise Tool, and—most important—how to follow what she called "a trail marked upon the heart."

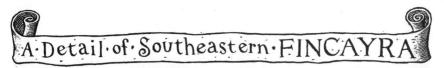

A·Detail·of·Southeastern·FINCAYRA

To THE DARK HILLS

be there Kreelixes?

Domnu's·Lair·
the·Galator·may·lie·here

THE HAUNTED MARSH

The·Wheel·of·Wye

hidden·caves

This·way·to THE RUSTED PLAINS

The·Legendary
Carpet·Caerlochlann
found·here

The·Region·of

THE·SMOKING·CLIFFS

Ancient·home·of·the·Mellwyn=bri=Meath·clan

IAN·SCHOENHERR

MCMXCVIII

Varigal

As the ancient capital of **Fincayra**'s first people, the giants, Varigal seems as old as the mountains that surround it. Indeed, the city dates back to the island's earliest days. Of all Fincayrans, only the hag **Domnu** is old enough to recall the day the first giants were carved out of the cliffs—and she remembers it only because she wagered **Dagda** that it couldn't be done. But she lost the wager. With help from **Gwri of the Golden Hair**, who glowed with the light of a star, and **Lorilanda**, who sang the magical chant of new life, Dagda worked all night long to carve a giant from the stony side of a mountain. When he finished, a great people, as well as their capital city, was born. That is why, thousands of years later, bards still sing, "Talking trees and walking stones; Giants are the island's bones."

 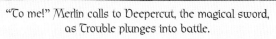

"To me!" Merlin calls to Deepercut, the magical sword,
as Trouble plunges into battle.

 Always a warm welcome for Rhia at her luminous home tree, Arbassa.

AVALON
WORLD BETWEEN ALL WORLDS

Strange Characters and Magical Terms

Abcahn ⪪

No one is more fluent in **Avalon**'s many languages than old Abcahn. His specialties include the whispered speech of the mist **faeries** and the exceedingly difficult underwater language of the mer people (which requires gurgling, humming, and bubble blowing—while trying not to drown). As a linguist, he is often asked to travel with the priestesses and priests of the **Society of the Whole**. His interest in language began during boyhood when he fell into a den of giant badgers and broke his leg. By the time he left several weeks later, wearing a splint that the badgers had made for him, he was fluent in *gruntsnarl*, their traditional speech.

In the Year of Avalon 987, Abcahn accompanied a group of Drumadians to **Waterroot**. When their boat was blown off course in the Rainbow Seas, into a cauldron of bubblefish, everyone on board became so giddy that they fell into the water and drowned. Only Abcahn survived, though not because of his wisdom or strength of will. No, he simply slipped and hit his head on the boat's side. He drifted, unconscious, until the danger had passed. Weeks later, he returned to the Drumadian compound with his tale of woe. Among those who heard it was **Lleu**, who later told it to **Elli**, **Brionna**, **Nuic**, and **Shim**.

Abelawn

The ancestors of Abelawn first settled in **Stoneroot**'s land of bells at the end of the Age of Flowering in **Avalon**'s third century. Abelawn continues the tradition of farming with Drumadian ethics—always seeking the consent of the goats, horses, and sheep who share his lands and labors. He is a friend of **Tamwyn**, and the young man often helps to harvest melons in the autumn, when there is little work for a wilderness guide. It was during one of those harvest seasons that Tamwyn dug up a dagger with most unusual markings—whose meaning he wouldn't fully understand until his battle with **Rhita Gawr** in the **stars**.

Aelonnia of Isenwy ⪜

Normally disguised as a mud-covered boulder, Aelonnia is much more than she seems. She is a mudmaker, one of the most mysterious and most magical creatures in **Avalon**. And she is the guardian of **Malóch**'s southernmost **portal**, near the Secret Spring of **Halaad**. Although she rarely shows her true form, she does so for **Tamwyn** and **Elli**, swelling to twice their height. She has enormous eyes, as brown as the rest of her body, and four slender arms, each with three long and delicate fingers that stroke the air continuously.

Aelonnia's whispering voice carries a lilt more like music than speech. And her words are full of wisdom about magic and its highest uses. For in the earliest days of Avalon, **Merlin** himself gave the mudmakers an extraordinary power—the ability to Make, to form living creatures from the élano-rich mud of this land. In the years since, the mudmakers have used this power judiciously, bringing to life creatures as varied as the giant elephaunts of Africqua and the tiny **light flyers** who accompany the **Lady of the Lake** wherever she goes. As Aelonnia explains to Tamwyn, "To Make, ten things we need: the seven sacred **Elements**, the mud that combines them, the time to do our work, and one thing more. The magic of Merlin."

Ahearna, the Star Galloper ⪜

"The great horse on high" of legend, Ahearna is a creature of the **stars**. She has massive wings, powerful legs, and a strong, rippling neigh. Her wings bear silvery white feathers that gleam as if made of starlight. Her deep brown eyes have seen much—including **Merlin** the wizard, whom she carried into the sky when he finally departed **Avalon** in the Year 694. Ever since that time, she has flown ceaselessly around a star known as the Heart of Pegasus. Just why is a secret known only to her and Merlin . . . until she shares that secret with **Tamwyn**.

Aileen

This young elf maiden is one of **Brionna**'s closest friends. Like Brionna, she grew up in eastern **Woodroot**, near the deepest forest of El Urien—and the rumored lair of the **Lady of the Lake**. Aileen lives in the highest tree house of a settlement built into the boughs of eight enormous elms. Unusually skilled as a carver, she is well on her way to becoming a master woodworker. More important to her friendship with Brionna, however, is Aileen's skill at brewing a tasty cup of hazelnut tea. Like most elves, she is a peaceful soul, although she could be convinced to fight for the survival of **Avalon**.

Angus Oge

This **fire angel** showed remarkable courage, as well as kindness, as he explored the farthest reaches of **Avalon**—so remarkable that he is remembered centuries later by Ayanowyn storypainters. As **Gwirion** explains to **Tamwyn**, Angus Oge gave so openly to the world that the world always found a way to give back to him.

Once, when Angus Oge was traveling across a distant realm, he lacked any food and was close to starvation. Weakly, he set his last remaining water to boil, hoping at least to make some thin soup from local plants. But he couldn't even find any leaves or roots that were edible. Just before he passed out from hunger, however, a wild hare bounded over and leaped right into the pot.

Arc-kaya

Her yellow eyes ablaze, this gray-haired eaglewoman healed **Scree** after he was badly wounded by a deadly shard from **Rhita Gawr**. Despite her fierce yellow eyes, her heart is deeply kind. Scree learns just how kind as he observes her helping others in **Stoneroot**'s Iye Kalakya clan. He also learns that she lost a son, named Ayell, when the young eagleman threw himself into the path of an arrow that had been shot at his mother. Irrationally, Arc-kaya blames herself for her son's death. She wishes, above all, that he were still alive to follow her clan's ancient blessing: "Soar high, run free."

Ayanowyn (Fire Angels)

The Ayanowyn people—the fire angels—live deep inside the trunk of the **Great Tree** (a region called the **Middle Realm**).

Inhabiting the caverns and tunnels near the upward-flowing **Spiral Cascades**, these people have painted the walls with spectacular murals that tell the story of their lives in **Avalon**. Theirs is a story that is truly glorious: Centuries ago, they traveled far rootward, to the realm of **Shadowroot**, and founded Dianarra, the City of Fallen Stars (called today the Lost City of Light). Yet their story is also truly tragic: As the fire angel **Gwirion** explains to **Tamwyn**, his people have declined terribly since the Age of Great Light, the Lumia col Lir.

Nothing reveals the fire angels' decline more clearly than their own withered forms. When healthy, their winged bodies flame bright orange with llalowyn, the fire of the soul. But when body and soul are ailing, as they are now, the fire angels can no longer fly—and resemble smoldering charcoal.

> *Any hope they may rise again is merely a spark blown upon the wind.*

The last seer of Gwirion's clan, the elderly woman **Mananaun**, prophesied that, one day, the fire angels would return to wisdom and glory. They would regain the power of their wings and the flame of their soulfires. Then, the seer proclaimed, they would fly back to the **stars** from whence they came long ago, in the time before storypainting began. The fire angels would be greeted by the great spirit **Dagda** himself. At that moment, their story would be renewed and they would gain, at last, their true name as a people. But when Gwirion first hears this prophecy, he dismisses it as wishful thinking. He is convinced that his people have fallen too far; he is sure that any hope they may rise again is merely a spark blown upon the wind.

Babd Catha, the Ogres' Bane

Never have the ogres of **Avalon** met a fiercer foe in battle than Babd Catha. While still a child in **Stoneroot**, she lost both her parents as well as her sister to marauding ogres. According to bards, the ogres attacked during a sudden snowstorm, and ever after, Babd Catha felt an irrational fear of snow. Even in her later years, as a famous warrior, it was said that she would stop fighting and retreat if even a single snowflake fell upon her.

Although she was very young when the ogres destroyed her family, and despite the fact that her own leg had been so badly injured that she would always walk with a limp, Babd Catha vowed to do whatever she could to prevent such tragedies from happening again. By the age of ten, she had become an accomplished swordswoman, and in that very year she fought her first ogre. While she was not able to kill the enemy, she did manage to frighten it so badly that it turned and ran off toward the high peaks of Olanabram. What distinguished Babd Catha was not just her ferocity, but also her tenacity—which is why she tracked that ogre for over two hundred leagues before she finally caught and killed it. Taking a lock of its hair, she wove the lock into her shirt, thus beginning a simple victory tradition that she would continue her whole life.

At thirteen, she had felled more than a score of ogres, usually during their attacks on human settlements. Although broadswords remained her weapon of choice, she also perfected the skills of wielding axes, maces, lances, and pikes. By her sixteenth birthday, she had collected enough locks of ogre hair to weave an entire shirt. That is why it surprised so many that she joined the new **Society of the Whole** as a follower of **Elen**. The following spring, in the Year of Avalon 18, she became one of the first priestesses ordained. She remained a friend of Elen, **Rhia**, and **Merlin** throughout her life. She was even invited to the wedding of Merlin and **Hallia**, but decided to battle ogres in **Rahnawyn** instead.

She lived a very long life, possibly due to a few drops of wizard's blood that Merlin once gave her to heal her wounds. Finally, she perished while saving the life of the great dragon **Basilgarrad** in the Battle of Fires Unending (chronicled in *Ultimate Magic*, the final book in the *Merlin's Dragon* trilogy). She bequeathed her entire collection of ogre hair shirts to the Eopia College of Mapmakers.

Basilgarrad, Wings of Peace

The greatest dragon ever to live in **Avalon**, Basilgarrad's name means *Basil the Great Heart*. His origins remain a mystery . . . although some believe that he sprang into being as part of Avalon—making him a living embodiment of his world. Others believe that he spent his youth hidden in a secluded place. But what place could have hidden such a huge dragon? Still others claim that he started out as a tiny, unremarkable lizard, although this theory is very difficult to believe. In any case, Basilgarrad's first known adventure was a great journey with **Aylah**, the wind sister. Soon he earned the name Wings of Peace by vigorously protecting smaller creatures who were bullied or attacked. In the War of Storms, he fought so courageously that he became a living legend. He angered many of his fellow dragons by siding with elves, humans, and eaglefolk in the centuries-long war. But he swiftly proved himself an extraordinary warrior, often defeating several dragons at a time—less through his vast size and strength than through his supreme bravery.

In time, Basilgarrad became a great friend of the wizard **Merlin**. It is said that the dragon actually saved Merlin from a deadly, magic-devouring **kreelix**—and that during the fight, the dragon suffered his first battle wound: a broken tooth. He possessed the unusual ability to cast smells over great distances (including his favorite smell, that of the herb basil). But as a green dragon from the western coast of **Woodroot**, he could not breathe fire. Even so, his sturdy scales shielded him from the flames of attackers. And his unusually broad wings gave him remarkable mobility in flight. His massive tail, though, was his most powerful weapon. "Brutal as the tail of Basilgarrad" goes the saying, for good reason. Yet this warrior could also be extremely gentle—as he proved to the female dragon who became the love of his life: **Marnya**, the only water dragon who ever learned how to fly.

When the War of Storms finally ended in the Year of Avalon 694—thanks to Basilgarrad's stunning victory over **Rhita Gawr** and his servant **Doomraga**—the great dragon carried Merlin all the way to the stars, so that Merlin could relight the darkened constellation known as the Wizard's Staff. After that journey, however, Basilgarrad mysteriously disappeared. Although many have pondered where he might have gone, no one is certain.

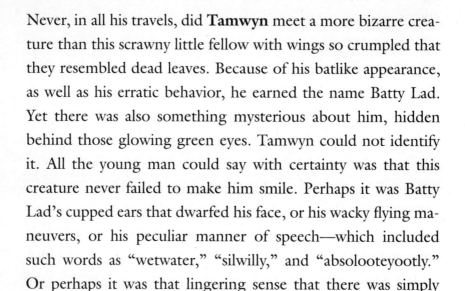

Batty Lad

Never, in all his travels, did **Tamwyn** meet a more bizarre creature than this scrawny little fellow with wings so crumpled that they resembled dead leaves. Because of his batlike appearance, as well as his erratic behavior, he earned the name Batty Lad. Yet there was also something mysterious about him, hidden behind those glowing green eyes. Tamwyn could not identify it. All the young man could say with certainty was that this creature never failed to make him smile. Perhaps it was Batty Lad's cupped ears that dwarfed his face, or his wacky flying maneuvers, or his peculiar manner of speech—which included such words as "wetwater," "silwilly," and "absolooteyootly." Or perhaps it was that lingering sense that there was simply more to Batty Lad than could be seen.

Bonlog Mountain-Mouth

The eldest daughter of the giant sorceress Jubolda, Bonlog has long been feared because of her violent temper—and also her huge, drooling mouth that constantly spills rivers of saliva. In the Battle of the Withered Spring, in the Year of Avalon 498,

Bonlog was saved by another giant, **Shim**, who accidentally crushed her attackers. Filled with gratitude, she tried to thank him with a kiss. But the mere sight of her puckering lips with rivers of drool terrified him so much that he shrieked in terror and dashed off into the mountains to hide. Humiliated, Bonlog Mountain-Mouth chased after him. Although she never caught him, a terrible thing did happen to Shim. For no explicable reason, he began to grow smaller and smaller, until he stood no taller than a young dwarf. Yet this misfortune did not diminish Bonlog's wrath: She continued to search for him, vowing revenge.

Brionna

As the granddaughter of **Tressimir**, the revered historian of the wood elves, Brionna grew up learning about the languages, customs, and stories of **Avalon**'s many peoples. She loved doing anything with her Granda—including traveling with him to other realms. The elf maiden even went with him to **Shadowroot** (where she nearly died from the sickness elves call darkdeath). Like other elves, she was raised to cherish all life. So she found herself in a terrible dilemma when she

> *She was stolen into slavery.*

was stolen into slavery and told that she must either help the wicked sorcerer **Kulwych**—or watch her beloved Granda die.

Brionna was slim, strong, and an expert archer, carrying a longbow made of springy cedar. A natural beauty, she wore her honey-colored hair in a long braid. And she was also feisty, with a very sharp tongue. Whenever her deep green eyes flashed in anger, it was time for others to beware, a lesson that **Scree** was especially slow to learn.

Brionna preferred to wear a loose-fitting robe woven from sturdy barkcloth, whose greenish brown color helped her blend into the forest. Often, she would sit or stand completely motionless, appreciating the many wonders of the woodland realm. In doing that, she found moments of great joy. Yet she also experienced times of great sorrow, and those memories sometimes felt even more painful than her wounds from a slave master's whip.

Catha

This silver-winged falcon is the **maryth** of the Drumadian priest **Lleu**, great-grandson of **Lleu of the One Ear**. Brave and bold, as well as intensely loyal, she is very similar in spirit to the hawk **Trouble**, who befriended **Merlin** ages ago. Appropriately, she is named for the famous warrior **Babd Catha, the Ogres' Bane**.

Ciann

A fire angel, Ciann belongs to the **Ayanowyn** people. But while he shares the same village with **Gwirion**, they have little else in common. Ciann may recall the glory of the fire angels' past and of their first great leader, **Ogallad the Worthy**, but he has forgotten the basic principles of his people. That is why he seeks power instead of redemption, ritual instead of meaning—which he shows when he tries to burn **Tamwyn** as a sacrifice on the clan's holy day.

Coerria (High Priestess Coerria)

Even as a young woman, Coerria struck the Drumadian Elders as wise beyond her years. Her serenity was such that her fellow priestesses dubbed her Quiet Island, since she held within herself a place of profound tranquillity. Now, at the age of nearly two hundred years, Coerria has grown frail in body, but that wisdom and serenity are as remarkable as ever.

As she strolls through the grounds and gardens of her beloved compound of the **Society of the Whole**, Coerria's long white hair is continuously straightened and braided by her **maryth**, a hive spirit named **Uzzzula**. As she moves, Coerria's elegant gown, woven of spider's silk, glistens, though not as brightly as her eyes. Those eyes are as blue as an alpine tarn. And they are no less observant for their years: Coerria is well aware of the personal ambitions of **Llynia**, just as she is quick to notice the potential of someone quite unusual—an apprentice third class named **Elliryanna**.

Cuttayka

To win the rank of first among the Clan Sentries, this burly eagleman with an angular jaw and sturdy wings had to prove his skills as a warrior. And he also needed to prove his loyalty to **Quenaykha**, the ruthless leader of the Bram Kaie clan of **Fire-root**. Cuttayka did both, many times over, as the battle scars on his chest proved. But as **Scree** discovered, Cuttayka gave his highest allegiance not to Quenaykha—but to the clan itself.

Deth Macoll

This master of disguise was **Avalon**'s most dangerous assassin—which is why the sorcerer **Kulwych** enlisted his services. Though human, Deth Macoll could alter his appearance almost as drastically as a changeling. He could appear, at one moment, as an elderly woman so hunched over that her head nearly touched her knees. Then, at the next moment, he could become a bumbling jester who wore tiny silver bells all over his clothes, so that he jingled whenever he moved. He could assume many other guises as well, although his true form was that of a bald man with a sallow face and flinty gray eyes.

More than the art of disguise, Deth Macoll enjoyed the sense of complete power he felt the instant before he killed someone. He savored that feeling, and often prolonged it by stretching out the death of his prey. As a youth, his parents disappeared just when his health deteriorated; during those years, what he most craved was a measure of control. Later in life, whenever he thrust his hidden blade into a new victim, he found exactly that.

Deth Macoll and Kulwych never enjoyed each other's

company. But they did sometimes work together because it was mutually profitable. When Deth was hired to hunt down the young priestess **Elli**, however, the old relationship suddenly changed. For their goal was not just to eliminate someone, but to gain enormous power in the process—power they would be unlikely to share.

Doomraga

Deep in the darkest part of **Avalon**'s most dreaded marsh, in a pit of rotting corpses, a terrible monster swelled in size—directly in proportion to the misery and suffering it had caused. Doomraga, surrounded by fearsome marsh ghouls, roared in rage as its body grew into a gigantic troll whose one red eye glowed ominously. For the arrival of its master, **Rhita Gawr**, was fast approaching, just as their long-awaited chance to conquer Avalon and crush the dragon **Basilgarrad** was also fast approaching.

Drumalings

Tamwyn first encountered these strange, treelike creatures in **Merlin's Knothole**, and then later in the branch-realm of **Holosarr**. Standing twice a man's height, their woody skin is knobby and weathered, with grassy tufts sprouting from their many limbs. Their faces are found midway up their scraggly forms: Each has a ragged slit for a mouth, a double knob that might be a nose, and a lone, vertical eye that is as tall and narrow as a twig. The eyes never blink. Drumalings, as Tamwyn learned from **Ethaun**, think not with words, but with emotions. And Tamwyn also learned, to his detriment, that those emotions often veer toward violent rage.

Edan ⇐

This wood elf is known for his skill as a tracker through the forests of **El Urien**. He is also known, as **Brionna** learned early in her childhood, for his temper. (His name, in the elvish tongue, means *fiery moods*.) Even so—like Brionna, **Aileen**, and other elves—he would not go to war unless **Avalon** was truly threatened.

Élano ⇐

The essential life-giving sap that flows within the roots, trunk, and branches of the **Great Tree of Avalon**, élano is a source of tremendous power. First discovered by **Merlin**, it seemed to him "the sum of all magic," a substance that held both power and wisdom. His staff, **Ohnyalei**, contained much élano, as did the magical **portals** throughout Avalon. **Lleu of the One Ear** was the first person to write about its life-giving power in his masterwork, *Cyclo Avalon*.

Elements (Seven Sacred Elements)

The seven sacred Elements of **Avalon** constituted the philosophical core of the **Society of the Whole**. In the words of the Society's founder, **Elen**, they were "the seven sacred parts that together make the Whole." Each of the Elements—Earth, Air, Fire, Water, Life, LightDark, and Mystery—inspired many treatises, ballads, and meditations. Together, they produced the life-giving power of **élano**, which flowed through every part of the Great Tree of Avalon. Because of that power, the Secret Spring of **Halaad** could heal any wound; **portals** could carry travelers to distant realms; and **Ohnyalei**, the precious staff of **Merlin**, could radiate wisdom. As **Aelonnia of Isenwy** explained to **Tamwyn**, her people's ability to create new life sprang from combining the Elements of Avalon with the magic of Merlin.

Elliryanna Lailoken (Elli)

One year after the dreaded Year of Darkness, Elli was born in **Mudroot**. A playful and resourceful child, she roamed with her father, a Drumadian priest who played the harp, and her mother, an herbal healer with extensive knowledge of the plants in the jungles of Africqua. Then, just before her tenth birthday, her life was torn asunder: Gnomes murdered her parents and stole Elli to make her a slave. For six brutal years, she lived in the gnomes' dark underground caverns, keeping herself alive (as well as sane) by playing her father's harp. Finally, she managed to escape. Having heard about the **Society of the Whole** from her father, she went to the Drumadian compound to learn the ways of **Avalon**'s founding spiritual guides, **Elen** and **Rhiannon**. By a mysterious coincidence, an ancient pinnacle sprite by the name of **Nuic** arrived at the compound simultaneously. Despite Elli's penchant for skipping her assigned duties, and her habit of missing formal prayers to meditate at the Great Temple whose

> *Elli's laughter was always as lilting as the song of a meadowlark.*

origins dated back to the **Dance of the Giants**, she was made an apprentice third class priestess. Nuic became her loyal **maryth**, though he refused to reveal his own past.

Despite her childhood losses and the trauma of slavery, Elli's laughter was always as lilting as the song of a meadowlark. Her brown hair, with curls as thick as a **faery**'s garden, surrounded her face, highlighting her hazel green eyes. While she had no idea that she would one day carry a gourd with magical healing water from the Secret Spring of **Halaad**, she had long carried something that was, to her, even more precious: her father's harp. The harp accompanied her everywhere—until the day she met **Tamwyn**.

From the first moment she encountered **High Priestess Coerria**, Elli revered the elder woman. Coerria's spirit seemed every bit as lovely, graceful, and unique as the shimmering

gown of spider's silk that she wore. Secretly, Elli admired the gown, which was made by the famous **Grand Elusa** of **Lost Fincayra**. But she was certain that she herself would never deserve to wear something of such beauty and heritage. Perhaps that was why she was so surprised when Coerria predicted that Elli would play a truly remarkable role in the future of the Society, as well as Avalon.

Ethaun

This brawny blacksmith looks more like a bear standing upright than a man. His muscular arms are as knotted as tree roots from working the bellows and forging tools; his chest is broad and powerful. Yet despite Ethaun's fearsome size, the gap-toothed grin within his gray beard reveals a friendly disposition. He is partial to expressions such as "tickle me toenails," and enjoys puffing on his pipe as he trades stories.

And he does have some intriguing stories to tell. As **Tamwyn** discovers when he meets Ethaun in **Merlin's Knothole**, high on the trunk of the **Great Tree**, the blacksmith actually traveled with **Krystallus Eopia**, Tamwyn's father, on the fateful expedition to the stars. As Ethaun explains, he learned a great deal about the famous explorer on that journey. But did he learn the secret of the magical torch? Or what ultimately happened to Krystallus? The answers to those questions may be surprising, as well as painful.

Faeries

Throughout **Avalon**, travelers hear the melodious hum of faeries' wings. It is a distinctive sound, common to all faeries. But to determine which variety of these creatures is making the sound, a closer look is required. Why? Because the types of faery folk are as varied as their habitats.

Water faeries have luminous blue wings, as lovely as translucent sapphires. They commonly wear silvery blue tunics, dewdrop-shaped shoes, and belts of dried berries. Parents will often carry their small children in backpacks made from periwinkle shells.

Mist faeries also wear blue garb—not tunics, but robes, jerkins, stockings, and sashes. Their clothing is a lighter shade of blue, tinted to match their wings, which are always a blur of motion. Their most recognizable feature, however, is the tiny silver bell that adorns each of their antennae.

Hedge faeries, by contrast, can be any variety of green and are covered with prickly fur. These faeries are famous for telling tall tales (and for stealing food from other people's gardens).

Starflower faeries have buttery yellow wings. Known for their artistic impulses, they often leave wreaths of brightly colored berries on tree roots and fern fronds. So it is not surprising that the greatest of all faery artisans, **Thule Ultima**, was a starflower faery.

Catnip faeries are recognized not by their coloring or clothing, but by their behavior: They are crazily wild. Watching them buzz about erratically, it is easy to understand the origin of the old saying "crazier than a clan of catnip faeries."

Mite faeries are found mainly in **Stoneroot** and are very small, even for faeries. A whole village of mite faeries could fit on **Tamwyn**'s thumbnail.

Dog faeries are obedient and hardworking. Some have walnut brown fur, white wings, and dangling pink tongues. (A team of eight of them is trained to pull the rope to ring the Buckle Bell at the Drumadian compound.)

Moss faeries look like tiny green humans with translucent wings. They enjoy tending moss, in gardens or in forests, and are often seen carrying water in hollow acorns.

Spray faeries, though smaller than most, are easily noticed because of their bright silver wings. These faeries love to congregate at waterfalls or fast-moving streams, glittering like liquid stars on the surface of the water. When they fly away in unison, it looks as if raindrops are rising off the water, raining upward into the sky.

Fairlyn

This tree spirit left her host tree, a lilac elm in the Forest Fairlyn, in order to become the **maryth** of **Llynia**. That constituted an act of great love, because it meant leaving behind her cherished homeland, a forest famed throughout **Woodroot** for its wondrous aromas. Fairlyn's boughs have no leaves, only rows of small, purple buds. But those buds produce a variety of fragrances, depending on her mood: If she smells like freshly picked rose petals, all is well; if she smells like freshly crushed bones, beware.

Fairlyn's special gift is to prepare a sensuous, aromatic bath. As **Elli** and **Nuic** discover, Fairlyn uses her many arms to mix and stir the liquids, powders, and pastes, even while her dark brown eyes scan her surroundings in search of any danger. Often, she enlists the help of **faeries**, who enjoy her fragrances—unless her mood turns sour, in which case the faeries quickly scatter.

Like all tree spirits, Fairlyn can live indefinitely, even after her host tree dies. Yet as she knows well, tree spirits can still die of grief or terrible wounds.

Fraitha

Fraitha is the sister of **Gwirion** of the **Ayanowyn** people. Like all fire angels, she is completely hairless. And like the rest of her people, who have lost the use of their wings, her soulfire burns so low that it no longer flames. Even so, as **Tamwyn** learns, there is still great bravery within her—as well as undiminished hope for her people. Fraitha, like Gwirion's wife, **Tulchinne**, often wears a heavy shawl woven from hurlyen, a sturdy red vine. She plays on an amber flute, which makes a deep, resonant sound that is reminiscent of the music of the **Spiral Cascades**.

Ghoulacas

These winged beasts were bred by the sorcerer **Kulwych** for just one purpose: killing his enemies. Although they are not very intelligent, they are dangerous—and are feared through-out **Avalon**, no less than the magic-eating **kreelixes** were feared in **Lost Fincayra**. The huge birds' wings and bodies are nearly transparent; only their bloodred talons and curved beaks are easily visible. Their screech is loud and terrible enough to freeze the hearts of their prey. Those who somehow survive their attacks, such as Kulwych's warrior **Harlech**, have scars to show for it. Because the ghoulacas' loyalty to Kulwych springs entirely from their fear of his wrath, there is always a chance that they might abandon him in the face of some greater terror. Even so, these killer birds are savage warriors who often battle to the death.

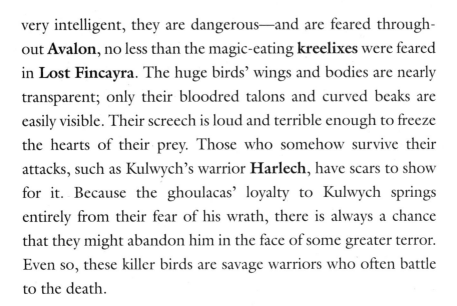

Grikkolo

Grikkolo, one of the last survivors of the dark elves' brutal civil war, lives in hiding amid the ruins of the ancient library of Dianarra, the Lost City of Light in **Shadowroot**. Slim and wiry, he resembles a wood elf (such as **Brionna**) in form. But his silvery gray eyes are quite different: They are very large, practically the size of a hen's eggs, and allow him to see well in the dark. His back is severely bent, causing his tunic to billow around his chest. From his head sprouts white hair as thick as a bed of ferns.

Grikkolo speaks in an erudite manner, for he is deeply learned. He is, as he explains to **Elli** and **Nuic**, always hungry—not for food but for information. That is why he originally came to the library. And why, although he has lived by himself for many years, he never feels lonely: He has countless friends—all the books that surround him. Yet he also cares deeply for the world outside his library. For that reason, even though he views himself as timid, he decides to do something extraordinarily brave to help Elli's quest.

Gwirion

Gwirion is a winged man with dark brown, shaggy skin that resembles the bark of a burned tree. Like the rest of the **Ayanowyn** people, the fire angels, his eyes are also deep brown. He whistles low, wandering notes when he is thinking. He is bald, like his sister, **Fraitha**, and his wife, **Tulchinne**. And his body temperature when

> *Gwirion is not actually overheated. He is, instead, far too cold.*

Tamwyn meets him—as they are fighting for their lives against giant termites—is so high that the young man thinks Gwirion is dying of fever. But Gwirion is not actually overheated. He is, instead, far too cold.

For the Ayanowyn people have fallen far. Their soulfires, called llalowyn, have dimmed so much that they no longer flame. Instead of the bright orange, winged beings they were long ago, when their great leader **Ogallad** led them out of the **stars** and into **Avalon**, they are now flightless creatures who resemble smoldering charcoal.

How did this happen? Greed and intolerance were the causes. As Gwirion explains, "We told ourselves that only we knew what was right and good. At the same time, we started thinking of the Great Tree as our land, our possession, to exploit and use however we liked. We grew wasteful, destructive, and shortsighted. We burned forests to clear land for grazing our captive beasts, even if it clogged the air and sullied our streams. Then we moved on to other forests and did the same, over and over again."

Gwirion longs for the return of his people's most wise and glorious days, the time before their decline. That time was known as Lumia col Lir—the Age of Great Light—and is revealed by the storypaintings in the caverns and tunnels of the **Middle Realm**. Even more, he longs for the flames of his own soulfire. As a child, he attempted to make his soulfire burn brighter by trying to swallow hot fire coals. He lost his ability to taste by doing so—but in all the years since, he has never lost his passion to burn bright.

Hac Yarrow

Long before **Scree** was born, Hac Yarrow was, along with **Ilyakk**, the most celebrated flyer in the history of the eaglefolk. The story is told that, only a few minutes after she was born in a nest on the ridges of **Olanabram**, this eaglegirl saw a cloud floating high above her. She reached for it, stretching her tiny arms skyward, but could not touch its fluffy form. So upset was she, the story goes, that she cried for several days on end. And the tears finally ceased only when her eagle wings appeared at last, much earlier than usual for eaglefolk. Immediately, Hac Yarrow leaped out of her nest, flew up toward the clouds—and rarely stopped riding the winds for the rest of her life.

When, in her elder years, someone asked her why she still kept flying, she answered crisply, "I haven't yet found that cloud."

Halaad

A young child of the mudmakers of **Malóch**, Halaad had only begun to learn the ways of her elusive people when she was brutally attacked by gnomes. Gravely wounded, she crawled to the edge of a spring that bubbled out of the **élano**-rich mud of the plains. The magical qualities of this water immediately healed her wounds. And so, in the Year of Avalon 421, the Secret Spring of Halaad was discovered. Although this spring has long been celebrated in the stories and songs of bards throughout **Avalon**, its exact location is kept secret by the mudmakers. In all the centuries since its discovery, only two other people are known to have found it. They are the great wizard **Merlin**, and a young man whom **Aelonnia of Isenwy** dubbed a true Maker: **Tamwyn**.

Halona

Although she was born a princess of the flamelons, Halona rejected some of her people's fundamental values: their fierce enthusiasm for battle, their admiration for the warlord of the spirit world **Rhita Gawr**, and their disdain for any other races of people, especially humans. When she saw a human explorer, **Krystallus Eopia**, about to be killed, Halona acted boldly. She rescued the man and guided him to safety. Then, unexpectedly, they fell in love. Ignoring the danger of the Dark Prophecy, they married and conceived a child during the Year of Avalon 985—the Year of Darkness. Halona and Krystallus named the child **Tamwyn**, which means *dark flame* in the language of the flamelons. Tragically, the family was attacked soon after Tamwyn's birth. Believing that Krystallus had been killed, Halona escaped with her son into the remote cliffs of **Rahnawyn**'s Volcano Lands.

High on those cliffs, a strange and wondrous old man saved both their lives. At the same time, he brought them together with a recently orphaned eagleboy named **Scree**, who became Tamwyn's adopted brother. As full of grief as Halona was about having lost Krystallus, she never told Tamwyn the identity of his father, fearing that the knowledge might put him in danger. Meanwhile, it pleased her deeply to see how well the two brothers bonded—exploring, playing, and wrestling without end. At last, Halona decided that Tamwyn was old enough to learn the truth about his past. But before she could tell him, a band of **ghoulacas** bred by **Kulwych** flew out of a **portal** and killed her.

Hanwan Belamir (Olo Belamir)

A simple gardener at heart, Hanwan Belamir has the weathered, dirt-crusted hands of someone who enjoys working with plants. He wears a simple gray robe with long, wide sleeves and many hooks and pockets for garden tools. Around his neck is a string of garlic bulbs; one thumbnail is broken from digging in the soil.

Yet despite his appearance, Belamir is also more than a gardener. He is a charismatic teacher, with a deep voice that is both resonant and comforting. His teachings about improved techniques for farming productively led to the construction of the village of Prosperity in **Woodroot**, a bountiful settlement that is walled off from the surrounding forest. But Belamir's teachings have extended far beyond agriculture. His belief in humanity's "special role" as Nature's "benevolent guardians" has led him to develop theories about humanity's rightful "dominion" over other creatures. Those theories, in turn, have spawned the Humanity First movement, which has grown increasingly self-righteous and aggressive. The movement has led to outright scorn for the **Society of the Whole**'s fundamental principle of harmony and mutual respect among all living creatures—just as it has led to violent attacks by humans against other beings.

> *No one since Merlin himself has been so revered.*

Although Belamir is reviled by the elves and others, his following among humans continues to grow. Some, in fact, have taken to calling him Olo Belamir, adding the ancient term of honor to his name. No one since **Merlin** himself, who won the name Olo Eopia, has been so revered. Yet Belamir himself scoffs at such attention, preferring to call himself simply "a humble gardener."

Hargol

Hargol, highlord of the water dragons, always wears a bejeweled crown of golden coral on his brow, along with immense earrings made from thousands of black pearls strung on braids of sea kelp. The earrings clink and clatter whenever he moves his head. Barnacles studded with jewels also decorate his enormous snout. Hargol's fiery green eyes are very watchful, and he has ears as large as the sails of elven ships. As is common with water dragons, his massive body is covered with scales that range in color from glacial blue to dark purple. He is, indeed, very large, at least four times the size of his guards, with a head the size of a fortress. When Hargol speaks within the central cavern of his lair, his words rumble like a crashing waterfall. So loud is his voice that the sea stars decorating the ceiling of his cavern often break loose from the vibrations and rain down on his guards.

Hargol's lair is deep in **Brynchilla**, amid the Rainbow Seas. As a direct descendant of Bendegeit, the brave highlord of the water dragons who rallied for peace in the War of Storms, he has a peaceful side. He is also deeply learned, and fluent in many languages; he is given to quoting adages from **Avalon**'s diverse peoples. But he can also be very dangerous (as **Elli** learns). Like all water dragons, when enraged, he breathes ice—vast torrents of blue-tinted ice. And like other dragons—with very few exceptions, such as **Merlin**'s friend **Basilgarrad**—he hungers for jewels and crystals of beauty and power. In fact, Hargol possesses a special ability: He can sense the location of crystals, even very far away, and he can also sense their magical powers.

Harlech

This hulking warrior carries an assortment of weapons on his belt: a broadsword, a rapier, two daggers, and occasionally an ax. He fears only one thing—the wrath of his master, the sorcerer **Kulwych**. On his jaw is a deep scar from an attack by deadly **ghoulacas**. And he harbors a particular hatred for the only person who ever bested him in battle, the mighty eagle-man **Scree**.

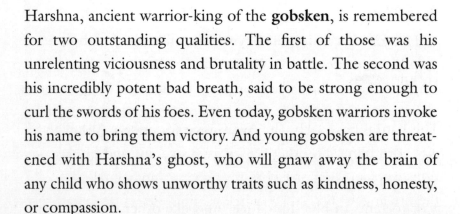

Harshna

Harshna, ancient warrior-king of the **gobsken**, is remembered for two outstanding qualities. The first of those was his unrelenting viciousness and brutality in battle. The second was his incredibly potent bad breath, said to be strong enough to curl the swords of his foes. Even today, gobsken warriors invoke his name to bring them victory. And young gobsken are threatened with Harshna's ghost, who will gnaw away the brain of any child who shows unworthy traits such as kindness, honesty, or compassion.

Hawkeen ⪦

This golden-eyed eagleboy was one of the few survivors of an attack on his village, home of the Iye Kalakya clan of **Stone-root**. When the attackers descended on his people's nests, built on a remote flank of **Hallia**'s Peak, young Hawkeen tried to fight back. But the battle swiftly ended, leaving many dead—including the village healer, **Arc-kaya**, and Hawkeen's mother, whose heart had been pierced by an arrow. At the clan's burial mound, the eagleboy sang in memory of his mother, in a voice that blended the plaintive call of a child with the screeching cry of an eagle: "O Mother, my ship, my vessel on high! You have flown beyond sight, beyond fears. I miss you beyond any tears."

As he finished, his gaze met that of the eagleman **Scree**, who had once lost his own mother to a murderer's arrow. In Scree's strength, Hawkeen found a touch of hope. And in the eagleboy, Scree found a reflection of his younger self. He recognized this sad but sturdy youth; he knew this mixture of anguish and resolve. The bond between Hawkeen and Scree would grow, so much that they would one day fight together at **Avalon**'s Battle of Isenwy.

Helvin ⪦

This bard is beloved by the **Ayanowyn** fire angels. Although he was born blind, his other senses were so acute and his descriptions were so vivid that Helvin's rich, entrancing tales inspired the fire angels' first storypaintings, the spectacular murals that now cover the walls of caverns and tunnels throughout the **Middle Realm** of the **Great Tree**. **Tamwyn**'s friend **Gwirion**, himself a storypainter, is most fond of Helvin's tales of **Ogallad the Worthy**. For those tales carry the hope that the fire angels might someday burn bright again—and possibly fulfill their dream of soaring up to the **stars**.

Henni Hoolah

Henni, whose full name is Henniwashinachtifig, stands half the height of **Tamwyn**. But he has more than double the young man's capacity for making mischief. As a hoolah, he has no sense of caution, no sense of honor, and no sense of dignity—basically no sense at all. To Henni, life is just a game. Any mischief is good fun; any danger is irrelevant. As he tells Tamwyn soon after they meet, "I've never met a death trap I didn't like."

Like other hoolahs, Henni has very large hands (good for climbing trees or hurling fruit) and silver eyes surrounded by circular eyebrows. He laughs easily—especially at Tamwyn's clumsiness—and releases a raucous "eehee, eehee, hoohoohoo-hahaha" that can be heard from one end of a forest to another. In the custom of his people, he dresses simply, wearing only a baggy tunic and a red headband, and carries a slingshot in his belt.

Something about Henni may be changing, however. Gradually, he seems more conscious of his actions, and he may actually be showing signs of concern for others. It may even be true that he is more aware of the value of life (including his

 Ever cloaked in shadow, Kulwych the sorcerer plots
revenge against Merlin and the world of Avalon.

 The Lady of the Lake approaches, surrounded
by mystery as thick as the magical mists.

own). Yet these changes may not last. And for now, at least, none of this is as meaningful to Henni as the simple fun of pelting Tamwyn with fruit—or pushing him into the **Spiral Cascades**.

Hywel

As the oldest of the Drumadian Elders, Hywel has lived in the compound longer than anyone else—including **High Priestess Coerria**, who is nearly two hundred years old. Hywel was a leader of the **Society of the Whole** before some of the current Elders were even born. As such, she takes very seriously her role as the keeper of the Society's traditions, through her responsibilities as the Dean of Timeliness and Decorum. After all, many of those traditions reach back to the days of the first priestesses, **Elen** and **Rhiannon**.

When Hywel stands beside the clanging Buckle Bell—which was made from the belt buckle of a giant, melted down by the breath of a fire dragon, molded by dwarves, and decorated by **faery** artisans—she wears woolen earmuffs to protect her hearing. But there is precious little hearing left to protect. Hywel's eyes, however, remain sharp. As she scans the newest crop of young apprentices, who are about to begin their formal prayers, she looks for any signs of disarray. What she does not expect is that one apprentice has skipped formal prayers altogether—for in all her years, she has never met anyone quite like **Elli**.

Ilyakk

No member of the eagle people, except possibly **Hac Yarrow**, loved to fly more than Ilyakk. And no other eagleman, except perhaps **Scree**, ever flew more courageously. As a young fledgling in **Rahnawyn**, Ilyakk decided to soar to the top of the highest volcano he could find. When that proved too easy, he rode the swells even higher, sailing over the Burnt Hills of the fire dragons. Finally, when he was too exhausted to fly any longer, he settled down for a rest—not on land, but on the scaly snout of an airborne fire dragon. The dragon, amused by this intrepid youngster, carried Ilyakk higher still, until at last they glimpsed the rumpled ridges of the **Great Tree**'s trunk rising upward. This experience merely whetted the eagleboy's appetite. As he grew older, he constantly pushed himself to fly higher and higher, rising to the Swaying Sea and beyond. No creature from the root-realms of Avalon—save only the great dragon **Basilgarrad**, who once carried **Merlin** to the **stars**—has ever flown so high as Ilyakk.

Imbolca

This Drumadian priestess, known for her perpetual scowl, is an ally of **Llynia**. She believes that the **Society of the Whole** must regain its original purity. As such, she is deeply offended by **Coerria**'s decision to admit **Elli** into the order, even as an apprentice third class. Imbolca's normally nasty mood always brightens a bit when her **maryth**, the ginger cat Mebd, scratches someone annoying.

Kerwin

Even as a young eagleman, Kerwin proved himself a warrior of great ability in many battles to defend the Tierrnawyn clan of upper **Olanabram**. Like his fellow eagleman **Scree**, Kerwin fought with supreme ferocity, but always within the bounds of honor. So it was no surprise that he was chosen to represent the allies of **Avalon** at the parley before the great Battle of Isenwy. Like the rest of his clan, Kerwin had skin as brown as the muddy plains, flashing eyes, and eaglefeathers marked with black stripes—as well as fierce devotion to his people's way of life.

Kree-ella

Kree-ella, an eaglewoman of the Bram Kaie clan in **Fireroot**, was bold enough to resist the murderous ways of the clan's leader **Quenaykha**. For this action, Quenaykha ordered her caught, tortured, and killed, then hung to a post as an example to other potential traitors. Such is the gentle temperament of the leader of the Bram Kaie—someone **Scree** must confront.

Krystallus Eopia

The boy who would become **Avalon**'s greatest explorer was born to the wizard **Merlin** and the deer woman **Hallia** in the Year of Avalon 27. Although he was almost crushed as an infant when the giant **Shim** tried to kiss him, Krystallus survived. Lacking his father's magical powers, as well as his mother's ability to run with the grace of a deer, he suffered from grave self-doubts. But from an early age, he demonstrated a strong passion for exploring. Blessed with an exceptionally long life, thanks to his wizard ancestry, he became the first person to explore many remote parts of Avalon, including the Great Hall of the Heartwood deep within the trunk of the Great Tree. Like his rival, the elf queen **Serella**, he developed considerable expertise in the dangerous art of **portal**seeking. He founded the Eopia College of Mapmakers in

> *All that seemed certain was that somewhere on his journey to the stars, this great explorer had perished.*

Waterroot, and chose for its emblem the star within a circle, the symbol for magically Leaping between places and times.

In the Year of Darkness, Krystallus journeyed to **Fireroot**. He was attacked by flamelons, but was subsequently rescued by the flamelon princess **Halona**. Despite the danger of the Dark Prophecy, they married and conceived a child. But soon after Halona gave birth, the family suffered a brutal attack. While

Krystallus managed to escape, he concluded that both his wife and their son, **Tamwyn**, had been killed.

Beset with grief, Krystallus embarked on his most ambitious journey ever—to find the secret pathway to the **stars**. Neither he nor any members of his expedition ever returned. By the time Tamwyn decided to search for his father, no one could say what route Krystallus might have taken to reach the highest realms. And no one could say what might have happened to his magical torch, a gift from Merlin, which continued to burn as long as Krystallus remained alive. All that seemed certain was that somewhere on his journey to the stars, this great explorer had perished.

Kulwych (White Hands)

As he prowled in the dark shadows of a stone wall above Prism Gorge in High **Brynchilla**, this cloaked sorcerer was all but invisible. Only his pale white hands could be seen: The fingernails were perfectly clipped; the skin bore not a single callus. The rest of Kulwych, called White Hands by some, remained hidden. But his actions were more easily viewed—whether by finding the disemboweled bodies whose entrails he had read, or by seeing the enslaved creatures whose lives he had destroyed. For the sorcerer had forced those slaves to build a massive dam across the gorge, a dam whose true purpose was known only to Kulwych and his master: the warlord of the spirit realm, **Rhita Gawr**.

Kulwych pulled the hood of his cloak tight around his head whenever the wind howled through the canyon, wishing he could return to his lair deep underground in **Shadowroot**. When, at last, **Tamwyn** made him remove his hood, the sorcerer's face looked more dead than alive. A jagged scar ran diagonally from the stub of what was once an ear down to his chin, taking out a chunk of his nose along the way. Where his right eye should have been, there was just a hollow pit, full of scabs and swollen veins. His mouth, burned shut on one side, was merely a lipless gash. Even so, as **Elli** and Tamwyn discovered, the most hideous part of Kulwych was not his face, but his mind.

Who had caused Kulwych's disfigurement? According to the sorcerer, it was **Merlin** himself, at the height of the War of Storms. Kulwych's will to live helped him survive, but brought him centuries of pain. During all that time, he plotted his ultimate revenge against Merlin—and against Merlin's beloved world of **Avalon**.

Lady of the Lake

Revered and dreaded throughout the realms, the Lady of the Lake first appeared in the deepest forests of **Woodroot** in **Avalon**'s sixth century. Where she came from, or how she gained her vast powers, no one can say. Even her precise location has never been confirmed. Of the many brave souls who have tried to find her, none succeeded and only a few ever returned.

Some people believe that the Lady must be a shape-shifting sorceress; others maintain that she is really the incarnation of the goddess **Lorilanda**. Still others claim that she is just an elderly woman who lives in a tree called New **Arbassa**, who surrounds herself with glowing **light flyers**, and who enjoys eating rivertang berries. Whatever her true identity may be, she remains shrouded in mystery as thick as the mists that swirl around her magical lair.

For reasons known only to herself, the Lady of the Lake has long favored the **Society of the Whole**. Yet even **High Priestess Coerria** only saw the Lady once, and that was in a vision. When the Lady appeared, aglow with blue light, she began by reciting the famous Dark Prophecy:

A year shall come when stars go dark,
And faith will fail anon—
For born shall be a child who spells
The end of Avalon.

The only hope beneath the stars
To save that world so fair
Will be the Merlin then alive:
The wizard's own true heir.

Then she revealed a secret—a secret about **Merlin** and his precious staff, **Ohnyalei**. Coerria told no one about this for many years. But that finally changed when she met a remarkable young apprentice priestess named **Elliryanna**.

Le-fen-flaith

Among the vaporous sylphs of **Airroot**, Le-fen-flaith is cele-brated as the realm's greatest architect. He designed many structures, including whimsical cloud sculptures viewed by appreciative audiences all across **Y Swylarna** in the seventh and eighth centuries of **Avalon**. He also perfected the first success-ful anchors for the strings of aeolian harps stretched between clouds. His most practical construction project was the bridge whose cloudthread ropes span the narrow gap between **Mudroot** and Airroot. Although the bridge was finally completed centuries ago, in the Year of Avalon 702, it has continued to stand—albeit shakily, as **Elli** discovered. The architect named it Trishila o Mageloo, which means *the air sighs sweetly* in the sylphs' native language. But in time, travelers came to call it the Misty Bridge. The first people to cross it, other than sylphs, were two special guests of Le-fen-flaith himself: the **Lady of the Lake**, whose eyes opened wide with wonder, and her good friend, the pinnacle sprite **Nuic**, whose eyes remained shut tight through the entire crossing.

Lleu

This tall, lanky priest of the **Society of the Whole** has sharp eyes crowned by thick, dark eyebrows. He is often accompa-nied by his **maryth**, **Catha**, a silver-winged falcon who likes to perch on his shoulder. Lleu was a good friend of **Elli**'s father, during their years together at the Drumadian compound, and is now one of **High Priestess Coerria**'s closest allies. Accordingly, he is deeply suspicious of the priestess **Llynia**, whose actions are guided more by her personal ambitions than her Drumadian principles. And he is willing to do anything to protect **Avalon**—even if that means facing the deadly changeling **Neh Gawthrech** in battle.

Lleu's great-grandfather, **Lleu of the One Ear**, authored the famous Drumadian text *Cyclo Avalon*. He was a good friend of **Merlin** and one of **Elen**'s original disciples in the earliest days of Avalon.

Llynia el Mari

Once she became the Chosen One, who would eventually become High Priestess, Llynia's arrogance and ambition began to overcome her devotion to the basic principles of the **Society of the Whole**. Not only was she the youngest Chosen One since **Rhiannon** herself, she possessed the gift of seeing visions of the future. Those visions may have been only occasional, and vague, but they were still enough to win her renown—and also to win her advantage in political schemes. As Llynia told herself regularly, she should use whatever means were necessary to climb to the highest levels of power. For she alone represented the purity of faith that could bring glory once again to the Drumadians.

Although she resented the efforts of **High Priestess Coerria** to humble her—requiring, for example, that Llynia wear the same simple greenish brown robe as other priestesses and priests—Llynia felt certain that she would prevail in time. She remained convinced of her own superiority even after a strange green mark appeared on her chin, the **Lady of the Lake** unexpectedly snubbed her, the lowly priestess **Elliryanna** outwitted her, and her devoted **maryth**, **Fairlyn**, finally rejected her. Fortunately, the wise teacher **Olo Belamir** appreciated her singular virtues, and proclaimed her Llynia the Seer.

Lott (Master Lott)

The only activities that Lott enjoys more than bossing around his roof-thatching laborers is eating a big, sumptuous meal—and then napping for several hours afterward. Having done much of both over the years, he is enormously fat. His eyes, sunk deep into the rolls of flab on his cheeks like a pair of almonds in a mound of dough, study his laborers suspiciously. Especially laborers such as **Tamwyn**—who, in Lott's view, is clumsier than a blind troll. Like many people who live in central **Stoneroot**, he often speaks in alliteration. Thus he shows his affection for Tamwyn by calling him "horrible hooligan," "lame-brained lout," and "sluggish scalawag."

Mananaun

The last seer of the **Ayanowyn** fire angels, Mananaun lived a long life. She died only eighty flames before **Tamwyn** arrived at the village of **Gwirion**'s clan, located near the upward-flowing

Spiral Cascades in the trunk of the **Great Tree**. Despite the misery of her people, whose soulfires had dimmed almost to the point of going out completely, Mananaun left behind a prophecy of hope. The fire angels, she predicted, would one day regain the power of their wings and the brilliance of their flames. They would fly back to the **stars**, where they had come from long ago in the days of **Ogallad**, and would be greeted by the great spirit **Dagda**. Then, at long last, the fire angels would gain their true name and their remarkable story would be renewed.

Marnya

The daughter of Bendegeit, highlord of the water dragons, Marnya spent her youth swimming, diving, and cavorting in the iridescent waters of the Rainbow Seas. Her luminous blue scales and azure eyes often gleamed in **Waterroot**'s waves. But this adventurous young dragon dreamed of doing something else, something no water dragon had ever done: She longed to fly. Finally, the brave dragon **Basilgarrad** showed her how. In return, she showed him the strength of her loyalty and the power of her love.

Maryths

Every priestess and priest in the **Society of the Whole** could count on the companionship of a maryth, whose loyalty would last as long as their lives as Drumadians. Inspired by **Merlin**'s friendship with the brave hawk **Trouble**, the Society's founders decreed that maryths could be any kind of creature but human. In the words of **Elen**, "Our friends, the maryths, will ensure that none of us will forget to open our ears to other songs—no matter how different the melody, or how

> *"Our friends, the maryths, will ensure that none of us will forget to open our ears to other songs."*

strange the rhythm." Consequently, maryths are as varied as the pinnacle sprite **Nuic**, the tree spirit **Fairlyn**, the bold falcon **Catha**, the irascible cat Mebd, and the hive spirit **Uzzzula**.

Maulkee

To **Quenaykha**, the eaglewoman who leads the renegade Bram Kaie clan of **Fireroot**, Maulkee is her most promising lieutenant. But to the eagleman **Scree**, who saw Maulkee kill the healer **Arc-kaya**, he is nothing but a bloody murderer. Maulkee is broad-shouldered and muscular, with a mouth that often twists into a haughty sneer. Though he is no more than seven years old, the eagleman is fully grown, the equivalent of a human in his twenties. And he is very experienced in the ways of warfare, a sport he quite enjoys. When he faces Scree in battle, both warriors feel unbridled rage—although Scree also feels a troubling hint of familiarity.

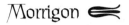

Morrigon

Despite his advanced age, Morrigon is spry enough to serve his master, the teacher **Belamir**, quite effectively. And he is also mean-spirited enough to encourage the violent excesses of Belamir's Humanity First movement. Although he looks rather frail, with scraggly white hair sprouting from his chin and both sides of his head, Morrigon is adept at archery. But it isn't his skill with the bow and arrow that arouses the elf **Brionna**'s curiosity. Rather, it is Morrigon's irritated eye, which is so bloodshot that it looks pink—unnaturally pink—the sign of a changeling.

Museo

Riding atop the head of the bard **Olewyn**, a museo is hidden under the bard's lopsided hat . . . until the time comes to sing. Then this small teardrop-shaped creature shows itself—more by its sound than its appearance. For like the others of its kind, the museo can sing with a rolling, layered hum that can entrance any listener. This rich hum contains many emotions, profoundly affecting anyone nearby. As the saying goes, "nothing is so deep as the note from a museo's throat."

Although museos can be any shade of blue or green, their skin is always flecked with gold. They are neither male nor female, but both at once. Museos have always been rare, even in their native land of **Shadowroot**. Centuries ago, they were driven out of the realm of eternal night. Since that time, they have wandered **Avalon**'s other root-realms with their chosen bards—always searching for the home they cannot find, always singing about the home they cannot forget.

Neh Gawthrech

Changelings are feared throughout **Avalon**—but no changeling is feared more than Neh Gawthrech. Known for the completeness of his disguises and the swiftness of his attacks, he changes so quickly that any witnesses see only a blur of claws, fangs, and the victim's blood. It is rumored that this changeling's true head is triangular in shape, with fangs that curl like scythes and scarlet eyes aflame with wrath. Last seen near the caves of the wyverns near the Wasteland of the Withered Spring in **Stoneroot**, he may have formed an alliance with the sorcerer **Kulwych**.

Nuic

This ancient pinnacle sprite from **Avalon**'s high peaks in **Olanabram** is small enough to ride on **Elli**'s shoulder. Yet just as his gruff, crusty manner conceals deeper emotions, his diminutive form conceals enormous wisdom and experience. Like all pinnacle sprites, he can produce a net of gleaming silver threads that serves as a parachute to float him down from cliffs. But his favorite pastime is more stationary: Nuic loves nothing more than to bathe relaxedly in a mountain stream, kicking his tiny feet in the water. An expert herbalist, he often forages for vegetarian foods and herbal remedies—then takes a long, cool soak afterward.

Precisely how old he is remains a mystery, though pinnacle sprites (like giants and dragons) can live for over a thousand years. The only mortal creatures who can live longer are wizards. Thus Nuic had many adventures before he became Elli's **maryth**. He became a valued friend of the **Lady of the Lake**. He was one of the first to cross the famous Misty Bridge of **Y Swylarna**. And he even attended the wedding of **Merlin** and **Hallia**, which took place atop the highest peak in the Seven Realms, in the Year of Avalon 27.

While Nuic's liquid purple eyes and green hair are striking, his most remarkable colors are those displayed by his skin, for they reveal his emotions. His skin fairly vibrates with colors, often in combination: orange for impatience, gray for somberness or gravity, red for anger, yellow for hunger, misty blue for contentment, and deep purple for pride. Two colors signify emotions so rare for Nuic that Elli was quite surprised when she noticed them—frosty white for terror, and flashing gold for amazement. And then, as she later discovered, there is one color even rarer: lavender, for pure affection.

Obba and Ossyn ⇐

Combined, the mental capacities of these two brothers equaled that of one barely functional imbecile. And their stupidity was exceeded only by their cruelty. Obba and Ossyn were hired by the sorcerer **Kulwych**, whom they called White Hands, in **Avalon**'s long-dreaded Year of Darkness. Their task: to find the child who was the true heir of **Merlin**. For that reason they traveled to the Volcano Lands of **Rahnawyn** . . . and to the nest of a fledgling eagleboy named **Scree**.

Ogallad the Worthy

Ogallad was the first great leader of the **Ayanowyn** people, the fire angels. Crowned by a golden wreath of mistletoe, a gift from the spirit lord **Dagda** himself, he led his people down from the **stars** long ago, in the days before storypainters began to record the fire angels' lives. Ogallad led the Ayanowyn to the **Middle Realm** of the **Great Tree of Avalon**—just as he led them to their age of wisdom and glory, the Age of Great Light known as Lumaria col Lir. Today, Ogallad's memory flames bright in the minds of **Gwirion**, **Fraitha**, **Tulchinne**, and **Ciann**—just as it did for the seer **Mananaun** and the blind bard **Helvin**. For that memory offers a hint of hope that those days of Great Light might somehow come again.

Olewyn the Bard

This strange old bard has a knack for appearing in the most unexpected places around **Avalon**. He looks bizarre, even comical, with a sideways-growing beard, a lopsided hat that conceals a genuine **museo**, and dark eyes that seem both very young and very old. Yet despite his appearance, quirky manner, and jaunty walk, there is something hauntingly serious about him. His name, Olewyn, is reminiscent of the legendary mer woman **Olwen**, who dared to leave her people and her ancestral home to wed **Tuatha** of **Lost Fincayra**. But that similarity could be just a coincidence: His name, like so much else about the bard, simply defies explanation.

Palimyst

Palimyst belonged to the Taliwonn people, the most remarkable creatures of the branch-realm **Holosarr**—and maybe of any realm in **Avalon**. When **Tamwyn** first met Palimyst, he realized that he must seem as strange to this creature as the creature seemed to him. (In fact, the name Holosarr was the Taliwonn word for *lowest realm,* since they had explored the higher branches of the **Great Tree** but remained completely unaware of the root-realms below.) Like the rest of his people, Palimyst was gigantic, standing twice Tamwyn's height. He had two brawny arms, a hunched and hairy back, and a single leg as thick as a tree trunk. By contrast, at the end of each arm was a hand with seven long, delicate

> *Palimyst was gigantic, standing twice Tamwyn's height.*

fingers, which Palimyst used for fine craftsmanship. His eyes were dark and intelligent, and he was quick to perceive the hope—as well as the heroic qualities—in Tamwyn. It was he who told the young man about the fabled **River of Time**, "the seam in the tent of the sky."

As a craftsman and collector, Palimyst lived in a tent of his own making. There he displayed objects that he had woven, carved, and sculpted. As varied as they were, those objects shared one fundamental virtue: All were made from natural materials shaped by mortal hands. Thus, as Palimyst explained, "they hold both the beauty of nature and the beauty of craftsmanship."

Tamwyn witnessed the strange, silent dance of Palimyst's people. They clasped their slender hands and formed a circle, hopping and bowing in unison. Despite their great size and their need to balance on one leg, they moved with all the fluidity of blowing clouds. And so, like everything else about these creatures, their dance was rich in remarkable contrasts.

Pwyll the Younger ⇌

Pwyll the Younger followed the path of his father, the poet Pwyll the Elder, and became one of the most famous bards in history. His songs and poems are as beloved by the people of **Avalon** as **Cairpré**'s were by the people of **Fincayra**. Particularly powerful were his ballads about human fallibilities: greed, arrogance, and intolerance. In contrast to his contemporary, **Willenia**, he held a dismal view of humanity, far more tragic than triumphant.

Quenaykha (Queen)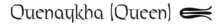

As the ruthless ruler of the Bram Kaie eaglefolk in **Fireroot**'s Volcano Lands, she preferred to be called simply "Queen." Under her leadership, the clan survived its most difficult time—but only by turning to thievery and murder. Discarding the eaglefolk's long-standing traditions of honor, this renegade group began to attack and pillage other clans. Instead of relying on their speed and talons in battle, the Bram Kaie used heavy wooden bows and arrows. The mere sight of their black-tipped wings and red leg bands was enough to prompt screeches of fear and outrage—as **Scree** witnessed during the attack that killed the healer **Arc-kaya**. And those screeches would have been louder still if people knew that Quenaykha had forged an alliance with the sorcerer **Kulwych**, who served **Rhita Gawr**.

But there was another side of Queen. It wasn't known by her followers, nor even her chief lieutenants **Cuttayka** and **Maulkee**. No, this side of her was known by only one person: Scree. For he had met her long ago, when she was still innocent enough to find joy in the sight of firebloom—the realm's only flower, whose orange petals resemble tiny feathers. Or was that only an act, a ploy to lure Scree into danger? Although he couldn't be sure of the truth, Scree concluded that he needed to do everything possible to stop the Bram Kaie's murderous ways. And so he decided to travel to their remote nests and challenge Queen for leadership of the clan. Even so, he had no idea what surprises—and trials—awaited him.

Ruthyn

No priestess in the **Society of the Whole** ever had a greater passion for the **stars**. She studied them day and night. Only **High Priestess Coerria** knew that Ruthyn's mother was one of the brave explorers who had joined **Krystallus Eopia** on his ill-fated journey to the uppermost reaches of **Avalon**—a journey from which no one returned. Whether she was searching for some sign of her lost mother, or simply for knowledge, Ruthyn became one of Avalon's experts on the history and lore of the constellations. But she, like everyone else, remained baffled by the enduring mystery of the stars' true nature.

Scree

"Bold" and "decisive" are often used to describe the eagle-folk—and they certainly describe Scree. Like the great flyers **Hac Yarrow** and **Ilyakk** before him, Scree was a daring master of the sky. Yet down inside, he always felt tormented by doubts about his capabilities and his true purpose in life. Born in a nest on the flaming cliffs of **Fireroot**, he knew only briefly the touch of his mother before she was murdered by men hired by the sorcerer **Kulwych** to find the true heir of **Merlin**. Scree was, on that night, too young to change at will into eagle form. So he could not yet sprout enormous wings from his human arms—wings with row upon row of feathers, entirely silver but for their tips as red as the volcanic fires of that realm. But he was not too young to remember every single word of his conversation with the mysterious old man who rescued him, along with **Tamwyn** and **Halona**. In the years to come, Scree would often reflect on what the old man had told him about the Dark Prophecy, the future of **Avalon**, and the precious **staff of Merlin**.

When in human form, Scree retained the hooked nose and pointed toenails characteristic of all eaglefolk, as well as large, yellow-rimmed eyes that could see with amazing clarity over vast distances. Yet his broad, muscular shoulders gave only a hint of his true potential. He could change instantly into eagle form, soar high among the clouds, and swoop down on a foe with ease, wielding his talons as an expert swordsman would wield his blades. When this winged warrior dived downward, he released a loud cry, part eagle and part human, that made most creatures run and hide. For that reason, he was greatly surprised by the elf maiden **Brionna**. She not only remained in place as he plunged toward her—but released an arrow that shot him out of the sky.

Scree's future remained as hard to read as the vaguely glowing runes on the staff that he once promised to protect. To find his way—and also to help Tamwyn, the young man he called "little brother"—he needed to discover the truth about his own past. That journey would lead him to confront the treacherous **Quenaykha** . . . as well as his own wounds that lay deeper than a talon's gash.

Serella

Even as a child near the headwaters of the River Relentless in **El Urien**, the elf Serella showed a strong penchant for exploring. At the age of two, she spent most of a summer stealthily watching a family of wyverns and learning their habits. (This was not easy, since one of their favorite habits was breathing fire on any living creatures they could find.) When Serella was seven years old, she built a small raft, packed her supplies, and floated down the river for a monthlong adventure. As worried as her parents were during her absence, when she finally returned unharmed, they recognized that she had shown remarkable courage and resilience. Rather than try to stop her from further explorations, they instead found expert tutors who trained her in wilderness traveling, mapmaking, and communicating in diverse languages. Their confidence in Serella proved to be well-founded, for in the Year of Avalon 51, she discovered a magical **portal** in eastern **Woodroot**.

Over time, Serella mastered the dangerous art of portalseeking, becoming the first mortal to survive such journeys through the inner pathways of the **Great Tree**. So strong were her leadership skills that she amassed many followers among the wood elves, who ultimately proclaimed her their queen. After deepening her knowledge of travel by portals, she led several expeditions to other parts of Avalon, including repeated journeys to **Waterroot**. These journeys culminated in the founding of Caer Serella, the first colony of elves in Waterroot, at a bay on the Rainbow Seas. Thus the society of water elves was born. In honor of Serella, and in memory of their origins, the water elves made their symbol a rainbow-colored wave encircled in forest green. Even today, that emblem graces the sails of all elven ships.

Serella continued her travels through portals, as did her fellow explorer, **Krystallus**. Although they spent many years as bitter rivals, a surprising turn of events brought them together as lovers. Often in the years to come, they could be found climbing sheer cliffs or trekking through uncharted forests— still competing with each other, but also enjoying their rich companionship. When, at last, Serella decided to return to **Shadowroot** to find the origin of the terrible disease darkdeath, Krystallus tried hard to dissuade her. But she went anyway. And when she did not return, he searched for her without success, ceasing only when she came to him in a dream and declared, "Explore the world while still you can! For that is the purpose of life and the reason for breath."

Society of the Whole

Founded in the earliest days of **Avalon**, the world-tree that sprouted from **Merlin**'s magical seed, the Society of the Whole became the supreme moral authority for Avalon's peoples. Under the guidance of **Elen** and her daughter, **Rhiannon**, the Society developed two basic principles: first, that all creatures should live together in harmony and mutual respect, and second, that everyone should help to protect the Great Tree that supported all forms of life. The new faith focused on seven **Elements**—what Elen called "the seven sacred parts that together make the Whole"—Earth, Air, Fire, Water, Life, LightDark, and Mystery.

With help from the great spirit **Dagda** (and several giants, led by Merlin's friend **Shim**), Elen and Rhia journeyed to **Lost Fincayra** to find the great circle of stones that was the site of the famous **Dance of the Giants**. Together, they transported the sacred stones all the way back to their compound in Avalon, and rebuilt the circle as their Great Temple. Soon thereafter, the Drumadians—as Elen called

> *The supreme moral authority for Avalon's peoples.*

members of the Society, in honor of Fincayra's **Druma Wood**— ordained their first priestesses and priests. They included **Lleu of the One Ear**, whose scholarly bent would lead him to write the Drumadians' classic text; **Cwen**, the last of the treelings; and (to the outright amazement of many) the warrior **Babd Catha, the Ogres' Bane**. Traditions flourished, and for centuries the Society thrived. The faith became as vibrant as the compound's many gardens and as solid as the famous Buckle Bell (which had been made from the belt buckle of a giant, melted down by the breath of a fire dragon, molded into shape by dwarves, and exquisitely decorated by **faery** artisans—as a symbol of unity and cooperation among Avalon's creatures). The Drumadians' most famous tradition involved **maryths**, lifelong friends of every priestess and priest who could be any kind of creature except human.

In time, though, the Society strayed from its ideals. Concerned with its own stature and power, it grew arrogant and rigid. This led to the abrupt departure of Rhia, who had succeeded her mother as High Priestess, in the Year of Avalon 413. By the time **Coerria** donned the silken gown of the High Priestess (a gown made originally for Elen by the **Grand Elusa**), the Society's troubles rivaled Avalon's. Indeed, the Society's very survival would require the courage, wisdom, and sacrifice of many—including Coerria, the tree spirit **Fairlyn**, the crusty old sprite **Nuic**, the star watcher **Ruthyn**, the priest **Lleu**, the hive spirit **Uzzzula**, and even the mysterious **Lady of the Lake**. But none of the Society's allies would play a more crucial role than a young apprentice third class named **Elliryanna**.

Tamwyn Eopia

His name means *dark flame*—fitting for someone born in **Avalon**'s realm of **Fireroot**, the son of the flamelon princess **Halona** and the human explorer **Krystallus**, in the Year of Avalon 985—the Year of Darkness that many feared would usher in the dreaded child of the Dark Prophecy. Even Tamwyn wondered which would be his true destiny: the dark or the light. Soon after his birth, flamelons attacked the family out of prejudice against people who mixed races. Krystallus survived, but believed that his wife and child had died. And so, filled with grief, he embarked upon the most dangerous expedition of his long life—to find a pathway to the **stars**. Halona and Tamwyn had actually escaped and hidden themselves in the Volcano Lands. When a strange encounter with a wondrous old man brought him together with an orphaned eagleboy, **Scree**, Tamwyn gained an adopted brother. Even in the years before Halona died in an attack by **ghoulacas**, the two boys were inseparable—until Tamwyn, at the age of ten, abruptly traveled by **portal** to the distant realm of **Stoneroot**. For seven years he searched for his lost brother, working as a wilderness guide and laborer, always keeping his age a secret because of the rampant fear of anyone who might be the child of the Dark Prophecy.

Though he was terribly clumsy, Tamwyn dreamed of becoming a great explorer. He longed to voyage all the way to the stars—to run among them, as if they were a radiant field. For ever since he could remember, he loved to run—losing his clumsiness in fluid motion that seemed almost as graceful as the bounding of a deer. Yet until he met the mysterious **Lady of the Lake,** he had no idea that this ability was the gift of his grandmother, **Hallia**, the deer woman of **Fincayra** who married the wizard **Merlin** in the earliest days of Avalon. Even then, Tamwyn suspected that he was more likely to be the child of the Dark Prophecy than the true heir of Merlin.

Always barefoot, Tamwyn had long black hair, with eyes equally dark. Over his shoulder he carried a simple pack, whose leather strap would one day have its own story to tell. He wore a small quartz bell on his hip, because its gentle sound reminded him of the land of bells. He also carried an old dagger, which he used mainly for whittling wood—unaware that it was actually connected, in a surprising way, to **Rhita Gawr**. Though his pocket always held a pair of iron stones and some grass tinder for making a campfire in the wilderness, he wondered whether he could discover the secret of making magical fire, just as he wondered whether the flame of his life would burn bright or dark. It would take all his courage, as well as help from the great spirits **Dagda** and **Lorilanda**, to discover the truth.

Thule Ultima

The greatest of all the **faery** artisans, this starflower faery with buttery yellow wings lived during the third century of **Avalon**. He carved the ornate oaken doorway to the residence of the High Priestess of the **Society of the Whole**, hovering over his work for weeks at a time without rest. He also perfected a technique for carving the nearly invisible bark of the eonia-lalo, **Airroot**'s tree of the clouds. But his most famous creations were musical instruments made from harmóna that he and his apprentices gathered from the forests of **El Urien**: That wood is so rich with musical magic that even the slightest breeze will cause it to vibrate harmoniously.

Tressimir

Before he became the elder historian of the wood elves, Tressimir witnessed many great moments in **Avalon**'s history. He helped **Krystallus** create the Eopia College of Mapmakers, rode on **Basilgarrad** into the Battle of Fires Unending, and was one of the few people who actually met the elusive **Lady of the Lake**.

But his life's greatest joy was something simpler: his bond

with his granddaughter, **Brionna**. She called him Granda, and they were each other's only family. He also shared Brionna's deep green eyes and pointed ears, as well as her ability to re-main utterly motionless in the forest. His robe, woven of green riverthread grass, often smelled like lemonbalm, which he used to ease his aching joints.

> *He hoped that his life might seem luminous.*

It was said among the elves that Tressimir could name every living tree in the forests of **El Urien**—and describe all the sights, sounds, and experiences that the tree had known throughout its seasons. He once confided to Brionna that, when it came his time to die, he wanted to be buried beneath one of those trees: an ancient beech tree known as Elna Lebram, whose name means *deep roots, long memories*. He hoped for a tradi-tional burial, where he would be wrapped in several layers of shrouds, woven from silverplume flowers, laurel roots, and leaves of everlasting. And he hoped that, on that day, his life might seem as luminous as the flames of the resinwax candles that elves would set afloat on a nearby stream—flames that, while very small, could still bring light to the darkened boughs above.

Tulchinne

For thirty-eight years, this **Ayanowyn** woman had been mar-ried to **Gwirion**, but she came to see him anew when **Tamwyn** entered their home. For this young man sparked her husband's hope. Like Gwirion and his sister, **Fraitha**, Tulchinne's soulfire burned very low. She wore a heavy shawl for warmth. Woven from hurlyen, a sturdy red vine, the shawl also covered her wings that were now—like those of all fire angels—too weak to fly.

Tulchinne loved to cook, and regularly served lauva, a traditional meal of the fire angels, in ironwood bowls. Although her husband was grateful for the delicious smells, he couldn't cook a successful meal himself. (This stemmed from the fact that he could not taste anything, having burned his mouth badly as a child.) Similarly, Gwirion often whistled, and Tulchinne enjoyed the music, but gave up long ago trying to master the art. "Whenever I try to whistle," she confessed, "small birds drop dead at our doorstep." Perhaps, Tamwyn muses, this arrangement helped their marriage: They filled each other's gaps, like two pieces of dovetailed woodwork.

Uzzzula

Resembling a bee with purple-tinted wings, this hive spirit was **High Priestess Coerria**'s devoted **maryth**. Known by all at the **Society of the Whole**, her language was a rhythmic mixture of hums, buzzes, and airy whistles. Uzzzula was often seen buzzing around Coerria's head, busily braiding the woman's long strands of white hair.

Willenia

Here was a bard who celebrated the wonders of her world! As exuberant as a meadowlark announcing the arrival of dawn, she wrote over five hundred poems and ballads. Willenia was revered by the people of **Avalon**, as was her more dismal contemporary, **Pwyll the Younger**. Yet much like **Cairpré** in the days of **Lost Fincayra**, this bard gave people a renewed sense of hope in themselves and their future. Willenia's cornerstone work was a complete history of Avalon, from the planting of **Merlin**'s magical seed through the ages of peace, war, and renewal that followed. Its opening lines, commonly called "Born of a Seed That Beats Like a Heart," are often sung by bards:

> *She wrote over five hundred poems and ballads.*

> As one world dies, another is born. It is a time both dark and bright, a moment of miracles. For even as Fincayra is saved, it is lost—passing forever into the Otherworld of the Spirits. But in that very moment, a new world appears. Born of a seed that beats like a heart, a seed won by Merlin on his journey through a magical Mirror, this new world is a tree: the Great Tree. It stands as a bridge between Earth and Heaven, between mortal and immortal, between shifting seas and eternal mist.
>
> Its landscape is immense, full of wonders and surprises.

Its populace is as far-flung as the stars on high. Its essence is part hope, part tragedy, part mystery.

Its name is Avalon.

Wondrous Places

Avalon (The Great Tree of Avalon)

Long ago, on the mist-shrouded isle of **Fincayra**, the young wizard **Merlin** planted a magical seed that beat like a heart. In time, it sprouted into a tree so vast and wondrous that it constituted an entirely new world: the Great Tree of Avalon.

Avalon is a world in between all other worlds, a bridge between mortal and immortal. Rooted in the mists of Lost Fincayra, it is a place of infinite wonders, with endlessly varied creatures and places. And Avalon became—for a time—the only world where humanity and all other creatures found a way to live together in true harmony. All of that changed

TO THE UNEXPLORED REGIONS OF
Upper Avalon:
TRUNK, BRANCHES, & THE STARS BEYOND
● Known Portals—
EVER FLOWS ÉLANO

Starward
N
W ● E
S
Rootward

SWAYING SEA (SITE OF THE TREATY ENDING THE WAR OF STORMS)

EL URIEN (WOODROOT)

HAUNTS OF MARSH GHOUL

SHRINE OF DAGDA
THE LAST SHOMORRA TREE
VILLAGE OF PROSPERITY

DEEP FOREST BEGINS

HALLIA'S PEAK
MERLIN'S STARGAZING STONE

JUNGLE OF AFRICA

INSTRUMENTS OF MUSICAL MAGIC CREATED HERE

WHITE GEYSER OF CRYSTILLIA
PRISM GORGE

HIGH PEAKS
LEGENDARY RUGGED PATH BE HERE?

RIVER RELENTLESS

HERE BE THE LADY OF THE LAKE?

THE SEVEN RIVERS OF COLOR

FOOTSTEPS OF THE GIANTS
DUN TARA SNOWFIELDS

LAKES

FOREST FAIRLYN

ARBASSA PASSAGES

AMENOU HOT SPRINGS

HIGH BRYNCHILLA

POOL OF STARS
WILLOW LAND

GREAT TEMPLE OF THE SOCIETY OF THE WHOLE

VILLAGE OF BELLS

BRYNCHILLA
(WATERROOT)

THE FLOWERING ISLES

WELLSPRING OF MIST
EOPIA COLLEGE OF MAPMAKERS

CAVES OF THE WYVERNS

OLANABRAM (STONEROOT)

RAINBOW SEAS
SEA OF SPRAY

TROLLDOOM: BEWARE

WASTELAND OF THE WITHERED SPRING

MARSHE...

The Seven Root-Realms of the Great Tree of AVALON

Born of Merlin's Magical Seed Planted in Lost Fincayra

T.A.B. '03 2003

GOBSKEN FORTRESS

CAVERNS OF THE FLAMING JEWELS

EVERNIGHT PEAKS

BEWARE OF DEATH DREAMERS

DOOMADAR LAKE

Vale of Echoes

lASTRAEL (SHADOWROOT)

DARK ELVES BE HERE

LOST CITY OF LIGHT

RAHNAWYN (FIREROOT)

VOLCANO LANDS

EAGLE FOLK BE HERE

CRATER OF THE CROOKED TEETH

RIVER OF FIRE

Hidden Gate

CLOUD GARDENS OF THE FAERIES

BURNT HILLS OF THE FIRE DRAGONS

FLAMELON FORGES

PALACES OF THE FLAMELONS

Hoolahome

DANCING GROUNDS OF MIST MAIDENS

MAELSTROM OF MYSTERY

Y SWYLARNA (AIR ROOT)

ANCESTRAL HOME OF MUSEOS

the Harplands

MALÓCH (MUDROOT)

MUD HILLS

WHISTLE POINT

PLAINS OF ISENWY

MUDMAKERS BE HERE?

MISTY BRIDGE

ISLES OF THE BIRDS

VEIL OF ILLUSION

THE SOUNDSWELLS

SHRINE OF LORI LANDS

CLIFFS PERILOUS

SECRET SPRING OF HALAAD?

HALL OF THE WINDS

Airfalls of Silmannon

GNOME LANDS OF THE LOWER MALÓCH

BIRTHPLACE OF SYLPHS

BEWARE OF BINKLES

CRAFTED FROM THE BEST AVAILABLE SOURCES YEAR OF AVALON 1002 BY the EOPIA COLLEGE OF MAPMAKERS

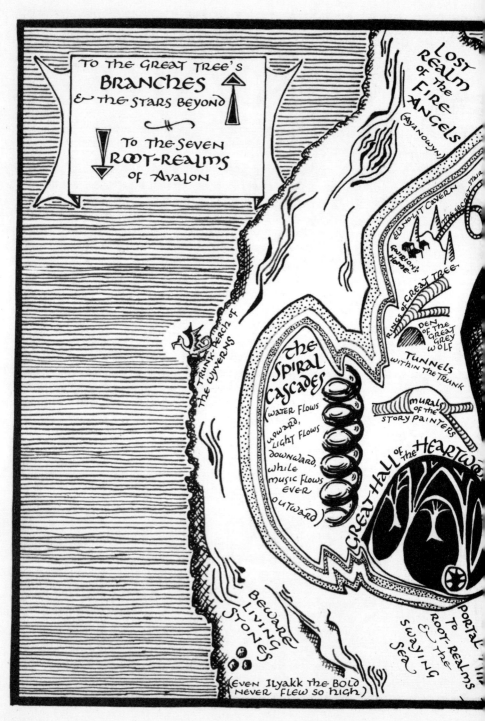

TO THE GREAT TREE'S
BRANCHES
& THE STARS BEYOND

TO THE SEVEN
ROOT-REALMS
OF AVALON

LOST
REALM
OF THE
FIRE
ANGELS
(AYANOWYN)

THE SECRET STAIR

GWIRION'S HOME

ETANO-LIT CAVERN

RINGS OF GREAT TREE

DEN OF THE GREAT GREY WOLF

TUNNELS WITHIN THE TRUNK

TRUNK-PERCH of THE WYVERNS

The
Spiral
Cascades

(WATER FLOWS
UPWARD,
LIGHT FLOWS
DOWNWARD,
WHILE
MUSIC FLOWS
EVER
OUTWARD)

MURALS of the STORY PAINTERS

GREAT HALL of the HEARTWOOD

BEWARE
LIVING
STONES

PORTAL to ROOT-REALMS & THE SWAYING SEA

(EVEN ILYAKK THE BOLD
NEVER FLEW SO HIGH)

LAST REFUGE OF ETHAUN

PRISM BIRDS SOAR HERE

MERLIN'S KNOTHOLE
KNOWN BY THE AYANOWYN AS NUADA ILBANA — WINDOW TO THE STARS

amon holm

T.A.B. © 2004

THE MIDDLE REALM OF THE GREAT TREE OF

AVALON

BORN OF MERLIN'S MAGICAL SEED PLANTED IN LOST FINCAYRA

STARWARD

N

W

E

S

where be the HIDDEN PASSAGE of KRYSTALLUS?

ROOTWARD

CRAFTED BY THE EOPIA COLLEGE OF MAPMAKERS FROM THE ANCIENT ANNALS OF THE AYONAWYN EXPLORERS

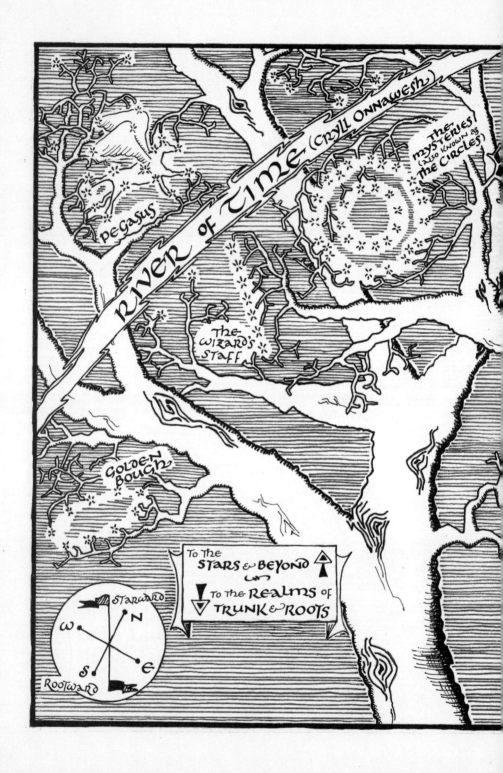

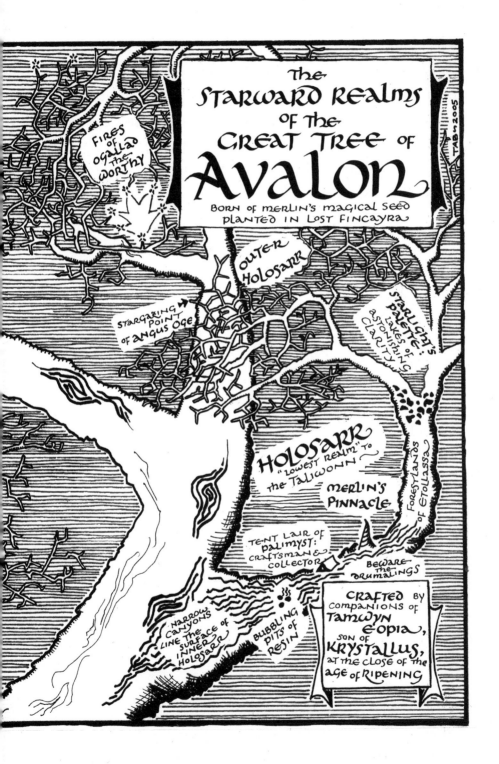

when human greed and arrogance grew too powerful. Then, as the **stars** on high began to vanish, causing the sky to darken, the future of the Great Tree darkened as well. Whether Avalon would be saved or lost, no one could foresee. Just as no one could tell who was the true heir of Merlin, destined to save Avalon—and who was the child of the Dark Prophecy, fated to destroy it.

Brynchilla (Waterroot)

Here is **Avalon**'s realm of water, where the smallest rivulets gleam with pure **élano** bubbling up from the depths of the Great Tree, and the largest rivers flash with currents of bright color destined for the Rainbow Seas. Everywhere in this realm is the sound of water—from the thunderous White Geyser of Crystillia to the melodious rainfall of the Sea of Spray. Many a bard has sung ballads about the Wellspring of Mist, the watery Willow Lands, or the magical reflections of the Pool of Stars, yet these are but a few drops in an ocean of marvels. Waterroot's creatures range from the joyous bubblefish, who live only as long as a single heartbeat, to the wrathful water dragons such as **Hargol**—who, when angered, breathe torrents of blue-tinted ice. Phosphorescence sparkles in the churning currents and the wakes of elven ships, whose sails are made from woven fronds of elbrankelp. Even the trees of this realm speak of water: Branwenna trees are so fluid that, when their bark is cut open, their liquid wood can be poured.

El Urien (Woodroot)

The forests of El Urien, the westernmost root-realm in **Avalon**, hold trees of every description, along with glades of infinite tranquillity. So it is no surprise that the realm's name means *deepest forest* in the wood elves' language. Here a traveler can find magical harmóna trees, whose wood vibrates melodiously with every breath of wind; lilac elms, whose boughs produce many sensuous aromas; and the rare Shomorra tree, which grows a different kind of fruit on every branch. This realm's most famous tree, however, is Elna Lebram, an ancient beech tree where the elves have buried their most revered bards and scholars, including the elder historian **Tressimir**. In addition to the wood elves, who live in elaborate tree houses, the forest is home to millions of **faeries**—mist faeries, moss faeries, star-flower faeries, and more. It is also home to innumerable kinds of food, including pears, tangerines, walnuts, spicy pepperroot, cherries, plums, almonds, and larkon fruit (whose taste, the wizard **Merlin** once declared, is like "liquid sunshine"). Wood-root is the chosen realm of the famous gardener and teacher **Belamir**, who lives in the walled village of Prosperity. Some-where in the dense woods lives another person, equally famous though far more mysterious: the **Lady of the Lake**.

Holosarr

Although it rests high above the roots and trunk of the **Great Tree**, Holosarr is **Avalon**'s lowest branch, far below the **stars**.

In fact, the name Holosarr is the Taliwonn people's term for *lowest realm*, since they have long been unaware of the root-realms below. (Hence the Taliwonn craftsman **Palimyst**'s astonishment when he first encountered **Tamwyn**.) Much of inner Holosarr, the region nearest the trunk of the Tree, is lined with long, narrow valleys divided by rocky ridges. Outer Holosarr, by contrast, is spotted with countless lakes of such clarity that they magnify the images of the stars. Because they also act like prisms, these lakes are called Starlight's Palette. In this realm live the Taliwonn people—immense, hunchbacked creatures who move with surprising grace despite the fact that each has only one leg. **Drumalings** also reside here, making any travel dangerous. High above soar colorful birds whose wingfeathers flash in the starlight, while bizarre insects fly nearer to the ground.

Lastrael (Shadowroot)

This is **Avalon**'s realm of eternal night. There is no dawn; there are no **stars**. In Shadowroot, light is an extremely rare phenomenon—to be deeply cherished or greatly despised, depending on one's view. Yet even in the unrelenting darkness, as the old elf **Grikkolo** would have pointed out, there are wonders of richness and subtlety. The **museos**, whose heart-rending music touches any listener, originate from this realm. So does ravenvine, which produces intense heat but no flames when burned. In the Vale of Echoes, a single footfall can sound like an army on the march; a single drop of rain, like an endless cascade. For a time, there was also a great city founded by **fire angels**, the ancestors of **Gwirion**: Dianarra, the City of Light, which hosted music and stories from many distant lands. The city flourished, adding radiant colors to the night, until a different form of darkness descended—the darkness of intolerance and fear.

Malóch (Mudroot)

The brown plains of this realm seem dreary and lifeless at first, since they contain mostly vast stretches of mud. Yet this mud, rich with sacred **élano**, holds extraordinary life-giving qualities. The elusive mudmakers who live in this region, including **Aelonnia of Isenwy**, wield magic that came from **Merlin**. They have long used this power to form new creatures from the mud—and the results range from enormous elephaunts to tiny, glowing **light flyers**. The Secret Spring of **Halaad**, full of élano, also bubbles out of these plains. But there is danger and brutality here as well, especially from the gnomes who live in underground tunnels. To the north, Mudroot erupts with greenery in the jungles of Africqua. Yet here again, surprising beauty exists alongside danger, since the haunts of marsh ghouls are not far away. Perhaps nowhere else in **Avalon** are there contrasts so dramatic as in Mudroot—so it may be fitting that this realm, so rich with new life, is also the scene of terrible slaughter in the climactic Battle of Isenwy.

Merlin's Knothole ⇐

"Window to the Stars" is what **Gwirion** called this place—
Nuada Ildana in the **Ayanowyn** tongue. As he explained to
Tamwyn, "It is an actual opening in the trunk of the **Great
Tree**—where the **stars**, not **élano**, are the source of light." The
Knothole lies at the highest starward point of the **Middle
Realm**. Because it juts out from the trunk of the Tree, people—
including **Ethaun**—can walk there, just as they do on the root-
realms below or the branches above. Most remarkable of all,
from this place one can easily view the branches . . . and all that
lies beyond. When Tamwyn finally arrives there, he will see all
these things, as well as one more thing that he did not expect
to find.

Middle Realm ⇐

This is the **Ayanowyn** people's name for the inner landscape of
the trunk of the **Great Tree**. Through the center of this realm
run the **Spiral Cascades**, which combine upward-flowing
water, downward-moving light, and outward-drifting music.
Emanating from the cascades are countless tunnels carved by
water, gnawed by termites, or opened by the workings of
élano. The radiance of this life-giving sap provides light to the
Middle Realm, making its tunnels and caverns glow subtly.
Many sections of the tunnels are decorated with spectacular
murals, created by Ayanowyn storypainters, while others reveal

colorful rings that hold the very memories of the Great Tree. High at the starward end of the realm is the Secret Stairway that leads to Nuada Ildana—Window to the Stars to the fire angels, and **Merlin's Knothole** to the famed explorer **Krystallus**. From that high perch, one can see the branches of the Tree and, beyond, the **stars of Avalon**.

Olanabram (Stoneroot)

Of all the root-realms, Stoneroot has the brightest starlight. No one knows why that is so, just as no one knows why Stoneroot's rocks change color with every season. The high peaks in the north include **Hallia**'s Peak, the tallest mountain in the Seven Realms and the only place where a traveler is high enough to see the lower reaches of **Avalon**'s trunk. In central Stoneroot's farmlands, bells are everywhere—on barn doors, weather vanes, barrels of ale, newborn lambs, and people's clothing. That is why this region is often called "the land of bells." Stoneroot's plant life ranges from the ancient, twisted spruces of the Dun Tara snowfields to the small, rounded cupwyll plants that grow all year round in rushing streams. The Great Temple of the **Society of the Whole** is in this realm, in the center of the Drumadian compound. Bards sing that the temple's stones came from the famous stone circle of the **Dance of the Giants** in **Lost Fincayra**, brought to Avalon with the help of **Dagda** himself.

Portals

Discovered by the wood elf **Serella** in the Year of Avalon 51, magical portals provide a very swift—and very dangerous—mode of travel throughout the root-realms of **Avalon**. While portals take varied forms, and are found in many different settings, they are always marked by crackling green flames. From the entrance to a portal, a traveler can glimpse what lies behind the flames: pulsing rivers of light that can carry people to any of the Seven Realms (except, in recent times, to **Shadowroot**, whose only portal was destroyed during the civil war of the dark elves). Portals also lead to the mysterious Swaying Sea, which is neither a root nor a branch, and—as the explorer **Krystallus** discovered—deep into the trunk itself, to the Great Hall of the Heartwood.

Portalseeking requires total concentration. For portals magically disassemble travelers, carrying them through the innermost veins of the Great Tree, and then reassemble them as they arrive at their destination. Without clarity of mind, travelers might arrive somewhere else—or, even worse, might disintegrate completely, merging utterly into the Tree's **élano**. And some portals seem to have minds of their own, choosing random destinations for voyagers. All this makes traveling through portals a delicate and dangerous art. In the words of Serella, "Portalseeking is a difficult way to travel, yet an easy way to die."

Rahnawyn (Fireroot)

Fireroot is **Avalon**'s realm of flaming ridges and charred rock, erupting volcanoes and plumes of sulfurous smoke. Most of this realm is red or orange; even its water is the color of rust. Ironwood trees, with fiber so hard they are fire resistant, flourish in the valleys. On the ridges of the Volcano Lands grow fire plants, shaped like ghoulish hands that grasp at the feet of passersby. Experienced travelers prize the honey of Fireroot's burning bees, which is always warm. (They work hard, however, to avoid the bees themselves, because their stings burn like hot coals.) Despite the harshness of the terrain, peculiar forms of wildlife abound. Salamanders enjoy lounging in flame vents, while oxen roam the Burnt Hills, always wary of fire dragons. Only one flower grows in this charred realm—firebloom, a small orange blossom that thrives on ground recently scorched by flames. The flamelon people are often, though not always, as fiery and volcanic as their homeland. They are industrious and inventive as well, with particular skill at crafting weapons of warfare. Most flamelons do not worship **Dagda** and **Lorilanda**, the great spirits of wisdom and rebirth who inspire many peoples throughout Avalon. Instead, they honor the wrathful spirit **Rhita Gawr**, seeing him not as a god of war, but as a force of creation that scours the land so that firebloom may flourish.

River of Time ⤳

A vague line of light in the sky, the River of Time is visible only from **Holosarr** or the higher branch-realms of **Avalon**. Like a luminous crack, or a seam in the fabric in the sky, it runs through the realm of the **stars**. In fact, the Taliwonn people of Holosarr have named it Cryll Onnawesh, which means *the seam in the tent of the sky.*

As the Taliwonn craftsman **Palimyst** explained to **Tamwyn**, the River actually divides the two halves of time—past and future. Thus within the River itself, time always remains fixed in the present. Because of this, anyone who enters the River can move along its course, which passes near every star, traveling enormous distances in space while remaining in the present time. And if Avalon indeed lies between all the other worlds, connecting each of them, then the River of Time links these worlds in a surprising fashion: One could ride to anywhere in the universe—and never leave the present moment.

Spiral Cascades ⤳

Flowing deep within the trunk of the **Great Tree**, this wondrous place is the union of three cascades. The first is made of water, which spirals higher and higher, connecting the roots far below to the **stars** high above. The second is made of light, which floats endlessly downward. And the third, as **Tamwyn** discovers, is made of music. The music vibrates, harplike, while swelling with the fullness of horns and the sweetness of bells.

Combined, the cascades spiral ceaselessly upward, downward, and outward.

Stars of Avalon

What, truly, are the stars of **Avalon**? That question has puzzled people through all the ages of this world. Many, like the young wilderness guide **Tamwyn**, have often gazed up at them, tracing the shapes of favorite constellations: Pegasus, soaring on high; Twisted Tree, stretching endless branches; the Mysteries, glowing with an aura of lavender blue; and the Wizard's Staff, burning bright for centuries after its stars were lit by the wizard **Merlin**.

Then, without warning, the stars of the Wizard's Staff darkened in the Year of Avalon 1002. One by one, as Tamwyn and others watched in stunned silence, their light vanished. For centuries, people had wondered why the stars dimmed at the end of every day, after a flash of golden light, and why they brightened again every morning. Now they began to wonder something else: whether the stars—and the world they illuminated—would ultimately survive.

Y Swylarna (Airroot) ⇐

In this airy realm of **Avalon**, cloudscapes seem to stretch forever, and aeolian harps play haunting music without beginning or end. Mist maidens spiral in their sacred dancing grounds,

faeries create cloud gardens, and the Air Falls of Silmannon rumble ceaselessly. Across the Misty Bridge, designed three centuries ago by the sylph architect **Le-fen-flaith**, the Veils of Illusion conjure images of whatever fears may be riding the wind. Not far to the north, the Harplands' vaporthread strings respond to travelers' deepest emotions, sounding discordant, harmonious, or conflicting mixtures of both. There are ghostly forests of eonia-lalo ("tree of the clouds" in the language of the sylphs), whose wood resembles frozen mist and whose bark is nearly invisible. Millions of winged creatures soar through this realm when they aren't resting at the Isles of Birds. Yet their songs are no more sweet, no more lilting, than the sounds of the airy realm itself.

 The ultimate battle for Avalon: High in the stars,
Basilgarrad fights the immortal Rhita Gawr.

Soulfires ablaze, the fire angels led by Gwirion join
Tamwyn and the great dragon Basilgarrad.

OTHERWORLD
THE SPIRIT REALM

Strange Characters and Magical Terms

Dagda

Dagda, deeply revered, is the god of supreme knowledge and wisdom. Together with **Lorilanda**, goddess of birth and renewal, he rules the **Otherworld of the Spirits**. As much as they savor the fruits of peace and serenity, they are always working to contain their nemesis, **Rhita Gawr**, who hungers to control all the worlds.

Bards sing that the young wizard **Merlin** traveled all the way from **Fincayra**, during the quest of the **Seven Songs**, to Dagda's Otherworld home at the mist-shrouded Tree of Soul. The great spirit appeared as an elderly man with a wounded arm—yet despite his frail appearance, his brown eyes seemed as bright as a sky full of stars. As he spoke with Merlin, he toyed with shreds of mist, knotting and unknotting them by a sweep of his finger or a mere glance. While Merlin had the distinct feeling that Dagda was doing much more than reshaping the mist, he also knew that the god would never interfere directly with the fate of mortal worlds. For Dagda believes profoundly in the importance of allowing mortals to choose their own futures, to create their own destinies.

That is why, more than a thousand years after that visit from Merlin, in the great battles for **Avalon**, Dagda resists the temptation to participate directly. Instead, he chooses to rely upon the courage, perseverance, and wisdom of mortals—especially two young people: a wilderness guide named **Tamwyn**, and an apprentice priestess named **Elli**. Joining them are many others, including the solitary eagleman **Scree**, the brave elf **Brionna**, the gruff pinnacle sprite **Nuic**, the irrepressible hoolah **Henni**, the wise craftsman **Palimyst**, the winged steed **Ahearna**, the loyal Drumadian priest **Lleu**, the shrunken giant **Shim**, and the ancient dragon **Basilgarrad**.

Lorilanda

Goddess of birth, flowering, and renewal, Lorilanda is allied with **Dagda** and is equally revered by the many peoples of **Avalon**. Together, Lorilanda and Dagda rule the **Otherworld of the Spirits**. While they greatly prefer times of peace, they must also fight to contain their nemesis, **Rhita Gawr**. For that warlord spirit desires one thing above all else: to control the realm of the spirits—and all other worlds, as well.

In the earliest days of Avalon, the image of Lorilanda often appeared, taking the form of a graceful doe who brought about important discoveries. One such appearance, in the Year of Avalon 33, encouraged a young lad named Fergus to find the only path (other than through **portals**) connecting the realms of **Stoneroot** and **Woodroot**. Perhaps Lorilanda is also watching over **Elli**, **Nuic**, and **Tamwyn** when they follow that very same path nearly a thousand years later.

Rhita Gawr

This powerful warlord of the spirit realm continually battles **Dagda** and **Lorilanda** for control of the **Otherworld**. Yet that is far from the extent of his ambitions. His true desire is to tear apart the threads of the universal tapestry, luminous threads created over many eons, and to weave them into his own design. Nothing less than controlling every mortal world will satisfy him. That is why he has long sought to conquer two worlds in particular: **Fincayra**, the island connecting mortal and immortal, and **Avalon**, the Great Tree whose branches touch every world.

Having failed to conquer Fincayra—thanks to the young wizard **Merlin** and his allies—Rhita Gawr turns all his attention toward Avalon. By the time of the dreaded Year of Darkness, he has won the allegiance of the sorcerer **Kulwych**, whose task is to obtain, through whatever means necessary, a pure crystal of vengélano—a substance with unlimited powers of destruction. Rhita Gawr has also gained the loyalty of some of Avalon's most battle-hardened creatures, including ogres, gnomes, trolls, changelings, and **gobsken**—as well as the flamelons, who worship him as a fiery god of renewal. In addition, he is rapidly opening the doorways from the Otherworld into Avalon—doorways through which he and his army of immortal warriors can invade. Then he can enter Avalon, taking the form of an enormous dragon as mighty as the famous **Basilgarrad**. Rhita Gawr is certain that he will triumph. For no one—surely not **Tamwyn**, whom he recognizes as the clumsy young spawn of Merlin—can possibly stop him.

Wondrous Places

Otherworld of the Spirits

The Otherworld is home to immortal spirits such as **Dagda**, god of supreme wisdom; **Lorilanda**, goddess of birth and renewal; and **Rhita Gawr**, god of war and conquest. It was beyond extraordinary that a mortal man would ever voyage to the Otherworld, especially one so young as the boy **Merlin**—but that was just what he did in the quest of the **Seven Songs**. To save the lives of the two people he loved most—his mother, **Elen**, and his sister, **Rhia**—Merlin found the secret pathway called the Otherworld Well. His journey was recorded in *The Seven Songs of Merlin*:

As I followed the Well deeper, something about the mist began to change. Instead of hovering close to the stairs as it had near the entrance, the mist pulled farther away, opening into pockets of ever-changing shapes. Before long the pockets expanded into chambers, and the chambers widened into hollows. With each step downward the many vistas broadened, until I found myself in the middle of an immensely varied, constantly shifting landscape. A landscape of mist.

> ---
> *To save the lives of the two people he loved most, Merlin found the secret pathway called the Otherworld Well.*
> ---

In wispy traces and billowing hills, wide expanses and sharp pinnacles, the mist swirled about me. I glimpsed deep canyons, running farther than I could guess. And great mountains, moving higher or lower or both ways at once. Strange shapes floated throughout, beckoning me to come nearer. And through it all, mist curled and billowed—always changing, always the same. Or was it really mist? Was it, perhaps, made not of air and water but something else? Something more like light, or ideas, or feelings? This mist revealed more than it obscured. It would take many lifetimes to comprehend even a little of its true nature.

So this was what the Otherworld was like! Layers upon layers of shifting, wandering worlds. I could plunge endlessly outward among the billows or travel endlessly inward in the mist itself. Timeless. Limitless. Endless.

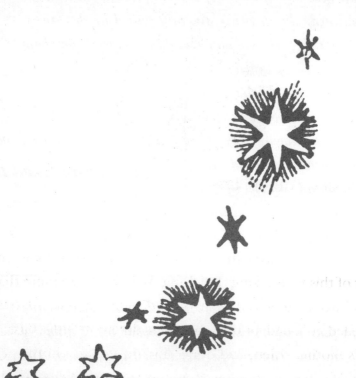

EARTH
HOME OF MORTALS

Strange Characters and Magical Terms

Arthur (King Arthur)

After the struggles, triumphs, losses, and gains of his **Lost Years**, the wizard **Merlin** was ideally suited to become the mentor of this young king. For King Arthur needed more than just guidance in how to rule a troubled realm on mortal **Earth**. He needed to build bridges between different faiths, just as Merlin's mother, **Elen**, had done, finding strength in the new religion of Christianity as well as the ancient religion of the Druids—along with the wisdom of the Jews, the Greeks, and others. He needed to communicate with royalty and aristocrats as well as craftsmen and peasants. He needed to speak the language of written texts as well as that of trees, rivers, and stones.

And he needed to understand the darker sides of humanity, which make us fall on our swords—as well as our lighter sides, which help us reach for the stars.

In Merlin, Arthur gained all this . . . and more. For Merlin taught this lad about courage, power, and honor—and even sent him (disguised as Ector) to the lost world of **Fincayra**. Most important of all, Merlin inspired Arthur to create **Camelot**, a new society founded on a radical ideal—the ideal of justice for all people. The wizard understood that, even if Camelot failed in its own time, it might yet succeed in a future time. As Merlin explained to his younger self, who had traveled to the future through Fincayra's magical Mirror: "A life— whether wizard or king, poet or gardener, seamstress or smith— is measured not by its length, but by the worth of its deeds, and the power of its dreams."

Excalibur

Never has a sword claimed a greater destiny than Excalibur. Wrought by the magic of **Merlin**, protected by the **Lady of the Lake**, and wielded by **King Arthur**, it represented the highest ideals of **Camelot**—ideals as indestructible as its blade.

Wondrous Places

Camelot

In this faraway realm on mortal **Earth**, young **King Arthur** joined his mentor, the great wizard **Merlin**, to create a new society based on the ideal of justice for all people. Although they knew that the realm might not succeed, Merlin declared, "A kingdom that is banished from the land may yet find a home in the heart." And that is precisely where Camelot has lived— and thrived—to this very day.

During his **Lost Years** on **Fincayra**, Merlin gained considerable wisdom, born of losses as well as gains, tragedies as well as triumphs. And he also found a sword—the sword that he would place in a stone for the future king. And so he brought to Camelot a true understanding of human weakness . . . as well as greatness. He also brought some rather unusual ideas for teaching the young king: He planned to turn Arthur into a fish, to teach him about power; and into a bird, to teach him to see beyond human boundaries. On top of this, he brought an ability to live backward in time (which he'd learned from **Gwri of the Golden Hair**).

As much as he had hated to leave Fincayra, his first true home, Merlin knew that this world held his higher destiny. He would always love Fincayra, and the newer world of **Avalon** that would grow from the magical seed he had planted just before departing. But Camelot, even as an idea, also claimed a piece of his heart. For Camelot could be, in time, a place of great hope and inspiration—a place that would honor the best in humanity, just as it would honor the land that people would someday call Merlin's Isle.

Earth

Homeland of humanity, Earth is a world of stark and subtle contrasts. It holds sublime beauty as well as horrid ugliness; it contains both mortal and immortal qualities; it knows both the short reach of human memory and the long reach of geologic time. There is war, poverty, and destruction of the very planet that supports all living creatures. And yet there is also natural wonder, diversity of life, and the most lovely expression of the human soul. Throughout history, humanity's qualities of creativity, compassion, generosity, courage, and wisdom have struggled against the darker sides of human nature: arrogance, greed, bigotry, ignorance, and hostility. In the end, the fate of this

> *The fates of these worlds may well be connected in surprising ways.*

world rests with humanity's ability to choose its own future, to create its own destiny, through free will.

In all these ways, Earth is perhaps not so different from the worlds of **Fincayra** and **Avalon**—worlds that exist in between mortal and immortal, physical and spiritual. And the fates of these worlds may well be connected in surprising ways. Perhaps that is why the greatest wizard of all times, **Merlin**, chose to make Earth his home. For despite its many troubles, Earth remains a place that inspires our highest hopes.

AVALON TIMELINE

Year 0:

Merlin plants the seed that beats like a heart. A tree is born: the Great Tree of Avalon.

The Age of Flowering

Year 1:

Creatures of all kinds migrate to the new world, or appear mysteriously, perhaps from the sacred mud of Malóch. The first age of Avalon, the Age of Flowering, begins.

Year 1:

Elen of the Sapphire Eyes and her daughter, Rhiannon, found a new faith, the Society of the Whole, and become its first priestesses. The Society is dedicated to promoting harmony among all living creatures, and to protecting the Great Tree that supports and sustains all life. The new faith focuses on seven sacred Elements—what Elen called "the seven sacred parts that together make the Whole." They are: Earth, Air, Fire, Water, Life, LightDark, and Mystery.

Year 2:

The great spirit Dagda, god of wisdom, visits both Elen and Rhia in a dream. He reveals that there are seven separate roots of Avalon, each with its own distinct landscapes and populations—and that their new faith will eventually reach into all of them. With Dagda's help, Elen, Rhia, and their original followers (plus several giants, led by Merlin's old friend Shim) make a journey to Lost Fincayra, to the great circle of stones that was the site of the famous Dance of the Giants. Together, they transport the sacred stones all the way back to Avalon. The circle is rebuilt deep in the realm of Stoneroot and becomes the Great Temple in the center of a new compound that is dedicated to the Society of the Whole.

Year 18:

The Drumadians—as the Society of the Whole is commonly called, in honor of Lost Fincayra's Druma Wood—ordain their first group of priestesses and priests. They include Lleu of the One Ear; Cwen, last of the treelings; and (to the surprise of many) Babd Catha, the Ogres' Bane.

Year 27:

Merlin returns to Avalon—to explore its mysteries, and more important, to wed the deer woman Hallia. They are married under shining stars in the high peaks of upper Olanabram. This region is the only place in the seven root-realms where the lower part of Avalon's trunk can actually be seen, rising into the ever-swirling mist. (The trunk can also be seen from the Swaying Sea, but this strange place is normally not considered part of the Great Tree's roots.) Here, atop the highest mountain in the Seven Realms, which Merlin names Hallia's Peak, they exchange their vows of loyalty and love. The wedding, announced by canyon eagles soaring on high, includes more varied kinds of creatures than have assembled anywhere since the Great Council of Fincayra after the Dance of Giants long ago. By the grace of Dagda, they are joined by three spirit-beings as well: the brave hawk, Trouble, who sits on Merlin's shoulder; the wise bard, Cairpré, who stands by Elen's side throughout the entire ceremony; and the deer man, Eremon, who is the devoted brother of Hallia. Even the dwarf ruler, Urnalda, attends—along with the great white spider known as the Grand Elusa; the jester Bumbelwy; the giant Shim; the scrubamuck-loving creature, the Ballymag; and the dragon queen, Gwynnia; plus several of her fire-breathing children. The ceremonies are conducted by Elen and Rhia, founders of the Society of the Whole, the priest Lleu of the One Ear, and the priestess Cwen of the treelings. (Babd Catha is also invited, but chooses to battle ogres instead.) According to legend, the great spirits

Dagda and Lorilanda also appear and give the newlyweds their everlasting blessings.

Year 27:

Krystallus Eopia, son of Merlin and Hallia, is born. Celebrations last for years—especially among the fun-loving hoolahs and sprites. Although the newborn is almost crushed when the giant Shim tries to kiss him, Krystallus survives and grows into a healthy child. While he is nonmagical, since wizards' powers often skip generations, his wizard's blood assures him a long life. Even as an infant, he shows an unusual penchant for exploring. Like his mother, he loves to run, though he cannot move with the speed and grace of a deer.

Year 33:

The mysterious Rugged Path, connecting the realms of Stoneroot and Woodroot, is discovered by a young lad named Fergus. Legend tells that Fergus found the path when he followed a strange white doe into the high peaks. Given how mysteriously the white doe appeared, she might really have been the spirit Lorilanda, goddess of birth, flowering, and renewal. The legend also says that the path runs only in one direction, though which direction—and why—remains unclear. Since very few travelers have ever reported finding the path, and since those reports seem unreliable, most people doubt that the path even exists.

Year 37:

Elen dies. She is grateful for her mortal years and yet deeply glad that she can at last rejoin her love, the bard Cairpré, in the land of the spirits. The great spirit Dagda himself, in the form of an enormous stag, appears in Avalon for the sole purpose of guiding her to the Otherworld. Rhia assumes Elen's responsibilities as High Priestess of the Society of the Whole.

Year 51:

Travel within the Seven Realms, through the use of enchanted portals, is discovered by the wood elf Serella. She becomes the first queen of the wood elves, and over time she learns much about this dangerous art. She leads several expeditions to Waterroot, which culminate in the founding of Caer Serella, the original colony of water elves. However, her final expedition to Shadowroot ends in complete disaster—and her own death.

Year 130:

A terrible blight appears in the upper reaches of Woodroot, killing everything it touches. Rhia, believing this to be the work of the evil spirit Rhita Gawr, seeks help from Merlin.

Year 131:

As the blight spreads, destroying trees and other living creatures in Woodroot's forests, Merlin takes Rhia and her trusted companion, the priest Lleu of the One Ear, on a remarkable journey. Traveling through portals known only to Merlin, they voyage deep inside the Great Tree. There they find a great subterranean lake that holds magical white water. After the lake's water rises to the surface at the White Geyser of Crystillia, in upper Waterroot, it separates into the seven colors of the spectrum (at Prism Gorge) and flows to many places, giving both water and color to everything it meets. Merlin reveals to Rhia and Lleu that this white water gains its magic from its high concentration of *élano*, the most powerful—and most elusive—magical substance in all of Avalon. Produced as sap deep within the Great Tree's roots, élano combines all seven sacred Elements, and is, in Merlin's words, "the true life-giving force of this world." At the great subterranean lake, Merlin gathers a small crystal of élano with the help of his staff—whose name, Ohnyalei, means *spirit of grace* in the Fincayran Old Tongue. Then he, Rhia, and Lleu return to Woodroot and place the crystal at the origin of the blight. Thanks to the power of élano, the blight recedes and finally disappears. Woodroot's forests are healed.

Year 132:

Rhia, as High Priestess, introduces her followers to élano, the essential life-giving sap of the Great Tree. Soon thereafter, Lleu of the One Ear publishes his masterwork, *Cyclo Avalon.* This book sets down everything that Lleu has learned about the seven sacred Elements, the portals within the Tree, and the lore of élano. It becomes the primary text for Drumadians throughout Avalon.

Year 192:

After a final journey to her ancestral home, the site of the legendary Carpet Caerlochlann, Hallia dies. So profound is Merlin's grief that he climbs high into the jagged mountains of Stoneroot and does not speak with anyone, even his sister, Rhia, for several months.

Year 193:

Merlin finally descends from the mountains—but only to depart from Avalon. He must leave, he tells his dearest friends, to devote himself entirely to a new challenge in another world: educating a young man named Arthur in the land of Britannia, part of mortal Earth. He hints, without revealing any details, that the fates of Earth and Avalon are somehow entwined.

Year 237:

Krystallus, now an accomplished explorer, founds the Eopia College of Mapmakers in Waterroot. As its emblem, he chooses the star within a circle, ancient symbol for the magic of Leaping between places and times.

The Age of Storms

Year 284:

Without any warning, the stars of one of Avalon's most prominent constellations, the Wizard's Staff, go dark. One by one, the seven stars in the constellation—symbolizing the legendary Seven Songs of Merlin, by which both the wizard and his staff came into their true powers—disappear. The process takes only three weeks. Star watchers agree that this portends something ominous for Avalon. The Age of Storms has begun.

Year 284:

War breaks out between dwarves and dragons in the realm of Fireroot, sparked by disputes over the underground caverns of Flaming Jewels. Although these two peoples have cooperated for centuries in harvesting as well as preserving the jewels, their unity finally crumbles. The skilled dwarves regard the jewels as sacred and want to harvest them only deliberately over long periods of time. By contrast, the dragons (and their allies, the flamelons) want to take immediate advantage of all the wealth and power that the jewels could provide. The fighting escalates, sweeping up other peoples—even some clans of normally peaceful faeries. Alliances form, pitting dwarves, most elves and humans, giants, and eaglefolk against the dragons, flamelons, dark elves, avaricious humans, and gobsken. Meanwhile, marauding ogres and trolls take advantage of the chaos. In the widening conflict, only the sylphs, mudmakers, and some museos remain neutral . . . while the hoolahs simply enjoy all the excitement.

Year 300:

The war worsens, spreading across the Seven Realms of Avalon. Drumadian Elders debate the true nature of the War of Storms: Is it limited exclusively to Avalon? Or is it really just a skirmish in the greater ongoing battle of the spirits—the clash between the brutal Rhita Gawr, whose goal is to control all the worlds, and the allies Lorilanda and Dagda, who want free peoples to choose for themselves? To most of Avalon's citizens, however, such a question is irrelevant. For them, the War of Storms is simply a time of struggle, hardship, and grief.

Year 413:

Rhia, who has grown deeply disillusioned with the brutality of Avalon's warring peoples—and also with the growing rigidity of the Society of the Whole—resigns as High Priestess. She departs for some remote part of Avalon and is never heard from again. Some believe that she traveled to mortal Earth to rejoin Merlin; others believe that she merely wandered alone until, at last, she died.

Year 421:

Halaad, child of the mudmakers, is gravely wounded by a

band of gnomes. Seeking safety, she crawls to the edge of a bubbling spring. Miraculously, her wounds heal. The Secret Spring of Halaad becomes famous in story and song—but its location remains hidden to all but the elusive mudmakers.

Year 472:

Bendegeit, highlord of the water dragons, presses for peace. On the eve of the first treaty, however, some dragons revolt. In the terrible battle that follows, Bendegeit is killed. The war rages on with renewed ferocity.

Year 498:

In early spring, when the first blossoms have appeared on the trees, an army of flamelons and dragons attacks Stoneroot. In the Battle of the Withered Spring, many villages are destroyed, countless lives are lost, and even the Great Temple of the Drumadians is scorched with flames. Only with the help of the mountain giants, led by Jubolda and her three daughters, are the invaders finally defeated. In the heat of the battle, Jubolda's eldest daughter, Bonlog Mountain-Mouth, is saved when her attackers are crushed by Shim, the old friend of Merlin. But when she tries to thank him with a kiss, he shrieks and flees into the highlands. Bonlog Mountain-Mouth tries to punish Shim for this humiliation, but cannot find him. Shim remains in hiding for many years.

Year 545:

The Lady of the Lake, a mysterious enchantress, first appears in the deepest forests of Woodroot. She issues a call for peace, spread throughout the Seven Realms by the small winged creatures called light flyers, but her words are not heeded.

Year 693:

The great wizard Merlin finally returns from Britannia. He leads the Battle of Fires Unending, which destroys the last alliance of dark elves and fire dragons. The flamelons reluctantly surrender. Gobsken, sensing defeat, scatter to the far reaches of the Seven Realms. Peace is restored at last.

The Age of Ripening

Year 693:

The great Treaty of the Swaying Sea, crafted by the Lady of the Lake, is signed by representatives of all known peoples except gnomes, ogres, trolls, gobsken, changelings, and death dreamers. The Age of Storms is over; the Age of Ripening begins.

Year 694:

Merlin again vanishes, but not before he announces that he expects never to return to Avalon. He declares solemnly that unless some new wizard appears—which is highly unlikely—the varied peoples of Avalon must look to themselves to find justice and peace. As a final, parting gesture, he travels to the stars with the aid of a great dragon named Basilgarrad—and then magically rekindles the seven stars of the Wizard's Staff, the constellation whose destruction presaged the terrible Age of Storms. At last, he departs for mortal Earth, by entering the mysterious River of Time from the branch-realm of Holosarr.

Year 694:

Soon after Merlin departs, the Lady of the Lake makes a chilling prediction, which comes to be known as the Dark Prophecy: A time will come when all the stars of Avalon will grow steadily darker, until there is a total stellar eclipse that lasts a whole year. And in that year, a child will be born who will bring about the very end of Avalon, the one and only world shared by all creatures alike—human and nonhuman, mortal and immortal. Only Merlin's true heir, the Lady of the Lake adds, might save Avalon. But she says no more about who the wizard's heir might be, or how he or she could defeat the child of the Dark Prophecy. And so throughout the realms, people wonder: *Who will be the child of the Dark Prophecy? And who will be the true heir of Merlin?*

Year 700:

In the eternal darkness of Shadowroot, a new city is founded: Dianarra, the City of Light. Legends say that the city was built by people from the stars, whose very bodies were aflame. Called Ayanowyn, or fire angels, they brought the light of torches and bonfires to Shadowroot. And another kind of light, as well—that of stories from many distant lands.

Year 702:

Le-fen-flaith, greatest architect of the sylphs of Airroot, completes his most ambitious (and useful) project to date: building a bridge, from ropes of spun cloudthread, spanning the misty gap between Airroot and Mudroot. He names it Trishila o Mageloo, which means *the air sighs sweetly* in the sylphs' native language. But in time, most travelers come to call it the Misty Bridge. The first people to cross it, other than sylphs, are the Lady of the Lake and her friend Nuic, a pinnacle sprite.

Year 717:

Krystallus, exceptionally long-lived due to his wizard ancestry and already the first person to have explored many parts of Avalon's roots, becomes the first ever to reach the Great Hall of the Heartwood. In the Great Hall he finds a single portal that could lead to all Seven Realms—but no way to go higher in the Tree. He vows to return one day, and to find some way to travel upward, perhaps even all the way to the stars.

Year 842:

In the remote realm of Woodroot, the old teacher Hanwan Belamir gains renown for his bold new ideas about agriculture and craftsmanship, which lead to more productive farms as well as more comfort and leisure for villagers. Some even begin to call him Olo Belamir—the first person to be hailed in that way since the birth of Avalon, when Merlin was proclaimed Olo Eopia. While the man himself humbly scoffs at such praise, his Academy of Prosperity thrives.

Year 894:

In Shadowroot, civil war erupts among the dark elves. When the fighting ends, most—if not all—of the dark elves are dead, the City of Light is destroyed, and Shadowroot's only portal to other realms is closed. What really happened remains a mystery that only the museos may fully comprehend.

Year 900:

Belamir's teachings continue to spread. Although wood elves and others resent his theories about humanity's "special role" in Avalon, more and more humans support him. As Belamir's following grows, his fame reaches into other realms.

Year 985:

As the Dark Prophecy predicted, a creeping eclipse slowly covers the stars of Avalon. So begins the much-feared Year of Darkness. Every realm (except the flamelon stronghold of Fireroot) declares a ban against having any new children during this time, out of fear that one of them could be the child of the Dark Prophecy. Some peoples, such as dwarves and water dragons, take the further step of killing any offspring born this year. Throughout the Seven Realms, Drumadian followers seek to find the dreaded child—as well as the true heir of Merlin.

Year 985:

Despite the pervasive darkness, Krystallus continues his explorations. He voyages to the realm of the flamelons, even though outsiders—especially those with human blood—have never been welcome there. Soon after he arrives, his party is attacked, and the survivors are captured. Somehow Krystallus escapes, with the help of an unidentified friend. (According to one rumor, that friend is Halona, princess of the flamelons; according to another, it is an eaglewoman.) Ignoring the danger of the Dark Prophecy, Krystallus and his rescuer are wed and conceive a child. Just after the birth, however, the mother and newborn son disappear.

Year 987:

Beset with grief over the loss of his wife and child, Krystallus sets out on another journey, his most ambitious quest ever: to find a route upward into the very trunk and limbs of the Great Tree. Some believe, however, that his true goal is something even more perilous—to solve at last the great mystery of Avalon's stars. Or is he really just fleeing from his grief? No one knows whether he ultimately reaches the stars. All that is certain is that Krystallus never returns.

Year 1002:

Seventeen years have now passed since the Year of Darkness. Troubles are mounting across the Seven Realms: fights between humans and other kinds of creatures; severe drought—and a strange graying of colors—in the upper reaches of Stoneroot, Waterroot, and Woodroot; attacks by nearly invisible killer birds called ghoulacas; and a vague sense of growing evil. Many people believe that all this proves that the dreaded child of the Dark Prophecy is alive and coming into power. They pray openly for the true heir of Merlin—or the long-departed wizard himself—to appear at last and save Avalon.

Year 1002:

Late in the year, as the drought worsens, the stars of a major constellation—the Wizard's Staff—begin to go out. This has happened only once before, other than in the

Year of Darkness: at the start of the Age of Storms in the Year of Avalon 284. No one knows why this is happening, or how to stop it. But most people fear that the vanishing of the Wizard's Staff can mean only one thing: the final ruin of Avalon.

INDEX

FINCAYRA

⤚ AVALON ⤙

OTHERWORLD

EARTH

T. A. BARRON is the award-winning, *New York Times* bestselling creator of the twelve-book Merlin Saga, which has sold millions of copies worldwide and has been translated into a dozen languages. Always a believer in the heroism of every child and in the magnificence of nature, Barron has become a major keeper of the Merlin story. Those same ideals led him to found the Gloria Barron Prize for Young Heroes, which honors outstanding young people of all descriptions.

He lives in Colorado with his wife and children, who are his favorite hiking partners and first readers.

Explore his website:
www.tabarron.com